D0796524

The Four Just Men

RICHARD HORATIO EDGAR WALLACE was born in Green-wich in 1875. He was brought up by a Billingsgate fish-porter and his wife, and attended an elementary school in Peckham until the age of 12. He worked as a newsboy, errand boy, milk roundsman, and labourer until the age of 18, when he enlisted in the Royal West Kent Regiment and served in South Africa. Discharged in 1899, he became foreign correspondent of the *Daily Mail*, but was sacked for involving them in a libel suit. His first great success was *The Four Just Men* (1905), in which readers were invited to solve the crime in return for a large cash prize (an embarrassing number guessed the solution). *The Council of Justice* (1908) and *The Three Just Men* (1925) were sequels. His early novels included a West African series, *Sanders of the River* (1911), *Bones* (1915) and others, but his thrillers and detective stories were the books that brought him enormous, lifelong popularity. Working with a dictaphone and a typist who held the record for speed-typing, he produced some 170 books, well meriting his nickname of 'fiction factory'. But he had an extraordinary talent for story-telling and for dia-logue, and his best works include *The Crimson Circle*, *The India-rubber Men*, *Room 13*, *The Fellowship of the Frog*, and *The Mind of Mr J G Reeder*. Wallace also wrote some excellent plays and an autobiography. He died in Hollywood in 1932.

JACK ADRIAN wrote his first book, a Sexton Blake thriller, in his early twenties. After seven years on the editorial side of IPC Magazines, he went freelance in 1975. He has written comic strip scripts, science fiction, and war, horror and mystery stories under a variety of pseudonyms and is an authority on twentieth-century popular and genre fiction. He is the editor of *'Sapper': The Best Short Stories* and *Edgar Wallace: 'The Sooper' and Others* (both published by J. M. Dent).

Edgar Wallace

THE FOUR JUST MEN

Introduced by Jack Adrian

J. M. Dent & Sons Ltd
London   Melbourne

First published in Great Britain in 1905
This paperback edition first published by J. M. Dent & Sons Ltd 1985
Introduction © Jack Adrian 1985

This book is set in 11/13 Linotron 202 Plantin by Inforum, Ltd, Portsmouth
Printed in Great Britain by Richard Clay (The Chaucer Press) Ltd, Bungay,
for
J. M. Dent & Sons Ltd
Aldine House, 33 Welbeck Street, London W1M 8LX

British Library Cataloguing in Publication Data

Wallace, Edgar
    The four just men.—(Classic thrillers)
    I. Title   II. Series
    823′.912[F]   PR6045.A327

    ISBN 0–460–02396–9

CONTENTS

INTRODUCTION

Jack Adrian

Consider this: After twenty years of misery, torture and degradation a famous and still influential black Nationalist manages to escape from a hideously repressive white-dominated regime. He flees to England, secure in the knowledge that in this country he will be safe from extradition. There is a political furore. The Home Secretary decides to push a Bill through Parliament changing the extradition laws so that the fugitive's immunity is destroyed; so that, indeed, he will be transported back whence he came, there to be either executed or imprisoned until he dies.

A group of young idealists—calling themselves, say, the Angry Unit—protest. This is, they proclaim, a monstrous crime against humanity; it must not be allowed to happen. The Home Secretary is unpopular, but not evil; for a politician he is a man of reasonable probity. He honestly believes that what he is doing is correct: that the presence of this man in this country at this time constitutes a danger to our democratic rights and traditions. The Angry Unit instigates a campaign of urban harassment. Super-glue is poured into post-boxes; statues are defaced; pictures are slashed in the National Gallery. This does not move the Home Secretary one jot. The Angry Unit issues an ultimatum: if the Home Secretary persists in his course of action he will be killed.

The Home Secretary persists. He is killed.

Forget for the moment the politics of the thing. Forget strict party lines and allegiances. Forget trigger-phrases such as 'Fascist state' or 'Left-wing extremists'. On whose side would we—that is, the generality of the populace—align ourselves?

I suspect that targets up to and including the National Gallery would, if viewed objectively, be considered fair, or fairish, game and would not engender much heat other than in the letters columns of the newspapers, and that only for a few days at a time. That is, feeling would certainly run against the so-called Angry Unit, and would progressively heighten as each new level of harassment were reached—but only as a sense of irritation changing to mild annoyance. Super-glue? Typical of today's layabout generation. The odd statue roughed up? That's what comes of abolishing corporal punishment in schools. Pictures slashed? Bring back National Service. On the whole though, nothing to get really worked up about; nothing here to destroy the fabric of society as we know it.

Murder of course would change all that. The Angry Unit would be reviled, anathematised, hunted down—however fine their cause, however noble their motives. The sympathy of the vast majority would instantly shift to the dead Home Secretary, his wife, his kith and kin. Probably, however unpopular the government under which he served, his political party as well. The shock-horror factor, even amongst those of the most liberal persuasion, would be enormous.

For there is no possibility of laughing murder off, or dismissing it in a newspaper cartoon or with a few grumbled curses aimed at the younger generation. Such a murder as this is the ultimate hint that the fabric of civilised society is indeed starting to tear, that chaos is only just around the corner. Only the hopelessly nihilistic, or the hopelessly insane, can contemplate murder—and especially murder as a political act—with equanimity.

And yet here, in Edgar Wallace's most celebrated thriller, we do just that. Indeed, we do more. We do not merely

viii

contemplate political assassination with equanimity, we applaud it.

In the book Manuel Garcia, leader of the Carlist movement and a political refugee, has fled from the clutches of the corrupt and brutal government of Spain to England (the year is 1904 or thereabouts). The Secretary of State for Foreign Affairs, Sir Philip Ramon, sets into motion a Bill in Parliament which, if passed, will effectively deliver Garcia into the hands of his enemies. A group of young idealists, calling themselves the Four Just Men, inform Ramon that unless he withdraws the Bill they will kill him. Ramon refuses to withdraw the Bill. The Four Just Men kill him.

This, in every way, is a heinous crime. The Foreign Secretary is shown quite clearly to be by no means an evil man, merely a bit of a cold fish. He is sarcastic, stubborn and unimaginative, and detests the general public. But he is also shrewd, zealous in his job, utterly incorruptible. His only crime is that he refuses to knuckle under to a bunch of terrorists.

The terrorists in question are like terrorists the world over and throughout history: vague, shadowy figures who flit from crime to crime and relentlessly deal death to eminent public figures: a judge, a prefect of police, the President of a South American republic, a one-time City Treasurer of New York, a well-known *grande dame* of French society. Shot, strangled or hanged. Sixteen murders in five years.

On the face of it a dreadful record, but of course nothing here is as it seems. The judge was a seven-times murderer, who used his position to massacre members of an opposing family in a bloody feud; the prefect was a 'notorious evil liver'; the President was a man of venal habits; the City Treasurer was an embezzler of public money; and of Madame Despard 'nothing good can be said'—she was a white slaver and procuress.

These then are the prime targets of the Four Just Men:

notorious evil livers and evil-doers whom the law, for one reason or another, cannot or will not touch.

> There were men, free of the law, who worked misery on their fellows: dreadful human ghouls fattening on the bodies and souls of the innocent and helpless; great magnates calling the law to their aid, or pushing it aside as circumstances demanded . . . There had grown into being systems which defied correction; corporations beyond chastisement; individuals protected by cunningly drawn legislation, and others who knew to an inch the scope of toleration. In the name of justice [the Four] struck swiftly, dispassionately, mercilessly. The great swindler, the *procureur*, the suborner of witnesses, the briber of juries—they died.

This apologia appears not in *The Four Just Men* itself but its sequel *The Council of Justice* (1908) but it perfectly epitomises the essential appeal of the Four Just Men.

For in an idle moment it's not such a bad idea. In every society in every age there are secret crimes perpetrated not only by individuals but great corporations, monolithic institutions, even purblind local governments. How wonderful to be rich enough and powerful enough and clever enough to take over that prerogative jealously guarded by governments since time immemorial: the power to administer law—the power to dispense a swingeing corrective to the secret criminals and those who massively but safely transgress; those who, in short, 'get away with it'.

The thought is strangely compelling, until one takes it to its logical, and chilling, conclusion. My secret criminals may not be your secret criminals. Indeed, my transgressors may be your heroes. And what if we both make mistakes? Better leave it all to fiction and the Four Just Men, who are dispassionate in their pursuit of evil and eminently fair. The odd Foreign Secretary excepted.

Not to mention, come to think of it, the odd pickpocket—for in the book a minor criminal, whose improbity on a Richter Scale of criminality amounts to about 0.1, is destroyed by the Four merely because he can identify one of their number. Not much justice there.

It is perhaps a measure of Wallace's particular genius that although his heroes murder these two relatively blameless characters we forget to censure them. Morality is tipped up on its head and we cheer. And deliberately tipped up, too: in a letter to his wife Ivy, written while in the white heat of creation, he mentions the pickpocket as 'a new character whom I introduced but to slay'. In another letter—his wife was in South Africa at the time, for a much-needed holiday from the ever-present threat of the bailiffs—Wallace set out his writing ambitions: 'I am going to give them crime and blood and three murders to the chapter.' Well, not quite that. Never quite that, even in the heady days of his greatest success a quarter of a century later when one in every four books bought in the United Kingdom was written by him. But what he did give the public in 1905 was certainly original, possibly unique—at least I can think of no other contemporary shocker that remotely resembles *The Four Just Men* in style, tone, plot or presentation.

As 'The Tallis Press' Wallace published the book himself. It was the first of many grandiose schemes for making pots of money without too much effort. At one time or another in later years, for instance, he produced a couple of racing-sheets and then bought himself into a somewhat shady tipster business; as 'R.E.H. Wallace' he created a 'general agents and merchants' company, whose business aims are still by no means clear; he put in with a friend to launch a sure-fire patent 'rheumatic-pad'; and with his long-suffering secretary Robert Curtis he started a number of competition-solution syndicates. None of these schemes succeeded but *The Four Just Men* had the best chance of any of them, had it not been for Wallace's inbuilt self-sabotage mechanism.

The novel was originally a puzzle-story. The solution to the mystery of how Sir Philip Ramon was murdered—in a locked and sealed room surrounded by an army of police—was not included in the original edition. A top prize of £250 was offered to the reader who came up with the right answer; another £250 was split up into consolation prizes. In 1905 £250 was a considerable sum, yet an initial outlay of 3/6d (17½p) was all that was required for a chance of carrying it off. And although the solution was ingenious (useable even today) it was also relatively simple, and very fairly clued. In a throwaway line Ramon says something important about himself; a pet hate is mentioned in the body of the text; a means of communication is briefly (14 words) alluded to; other hints are dropped, all pointing to the correct solution. With a reasonable amount of publicity the book ought to have brought in an immodest return.

But Wallace, recklessly extravagant even at the start of his career, launched a massive promotional campaign, and although he sold something approaching 40,000 copies of the book he soon discovered that he'd spent far more than he could ever earn. In the end he had to be baled out by *Daily Mail* proprietor Alfred Harmsworth to the tune of £1000. Still, as a piece of presentation it was clever and imaginative; certainly unique.

It is said that Wallace initially tried to interest other publishers in the book, but failed. If this is so, it is easy to see why. *The Four Just Men* as it stands is a very short book, hardly more than 40,000 words long. The major publishers needed to sell most of their initial print-run of any book to the circulating libraries such as Mudie's or W.H. Smith's, and no library would contemplate purchasing large quantities of what amounted to a novella by a new and untried author.

Especially a novella about the cold-blooded murder of a British Cabinet Minister in which the assassins get away scot-free. It smacked too much of the dreadful reality of the Fenian and Anarchist outrages of the 1880s and '90s.

Those outrages are surely what suggested to Wallace the basic plot of his story. They certainly provided plots for a good many of his peers. There was J. S. Fletcher's *The Three Days' Terror* (1901: anarchists hold London to ransom); Coulson Kernahan's *Captain Shannon* (1897: Fenians bomb London) and *Scoundrels & Co* (1900: anarchists—all, oddly, resembling Toulouse-Lautrec—loot London); and any number of shockers by George Griffith in which Nihilists, ladies of the British aristocracy, and piratical industrialists attempt various kinds of world domination or destruction. Wallace would doubtless have read most of these best-sellers, and others, and from them would have gauged what was acceptable to the reading public. And yet he went his own way. His characters defend the rights of the anarchists, and instead of some bright and sturdy young busybody defeating the Four in the end, it is the Four who quite literally get away with murder.

The concept of the outlaw-hero was nothing new and the late nineteenth century in particular saw a proliferation of the breed, especially in the world of the penny blood—sparked off by Harrison Ainsworth's clever sanctification of Dick Turpin in *Rookwood*. But in reality Turpin, Claude Duval, Robin Hood and the rest were at best scallywags, at worst gross thugs. Wallace, single-handed, created what the critic and authority on American pulp fiction Robert Sampson calls the Justice Figure—the 'incorruptible agent for justice' who deals death to evil-doers and is, because of this, pursued by the very law he seeks to uphold. Ironically, in novels such as *The Four Just Men* and *The Council of Justice* Wallace, who always yearned for American acceptance but only got it in the last decade of his life, was writing purely American-style pulp-magazine stories a quarter of a century before the genre existed.

But perhaps it is the style and tone of *The Four Just Men* which more than anything else make it so singular a thriller when compared with the circulating library sultans of the time. Try Headon Hill, try William le Queux; dip into, if you can, Fergus Hume or any of the six-bob shockers by the enormously prolific Guy Boothby (fifty-odd books in ten years). Grapple with the sensational novels of Dick Donovan, or Richard Marsh, or Hugh Conway, B. L. Farjeon, Hume Nisbet, even Phillips Oppenheim (at least from this period). All are more or less leaden in style and content.

By comparison *The Four Just Men*—originally published 80 years ago, almost to the month—is immensely, astonishingly readable. There is not a chapter, not a paragraph, not a sentence that bears even the slightest whiff of that late nineteenth-century mustiness that characterises even the best of its contemporaries. It is thumpingly twentieth century.

Wallace was one of Alfred Harmsworth's 'young men', one of the new breed of journalists who turned the *Daily Mail* into a paper that had (so Harmsworth boasted) six times the circulation of its nearest rival. In the *Daily Mail* offices there were large notices which read 'Paragraph! Paragraph! Paragraph!' Journalists were forced to write a good simple demotic prose and Wallace found he was a master at it. He also had a natural talent for the colourful vignette, and his descriptive pieces from this period—of train smashes, coal strikes, royal weddings—make marvellous, compelling reading. Even his despatches from South Africa, written during the Boer War and his first journalistic assignments, are full of life and vigour. To be sure, he was a hopeless reporter—hard news bored him, facts and figures were an irritation—but if a job required atmosphere, colour, the broad descriptive sweep, there were few who could equal Edgar Wallace even on a bad day.

Wallace brought his considerable journalistic skills to the writing of fiction and for better or worse they give all his books—even those written at a hectic pace—a quite distinctive character. Rarely were these talents used to greater effect than in *The Four Just Men*. Characters are neatly and economically sketched in; all come briskly to life. Falmouth, the police superintendent, is an overworked professional, cynical, abrasive (he once 'brusquely explained to a Royal Personage that he hadn't got eyes in the back of his head'). George Manfred, Leon Gonsalez and Raymond Poiccart, the Just Men themselves (the fourth, Miguel Thery, *alias* Saimont, was coopted for the job) are by no means remote and passionless supermen; even Manfred, their nominal leader, can lose his self-control in a sudden, shocking, emotional outburst. And Ramon, in a sense the most important character in the book, is deftly and convincingly portrayed throughout (a nice touch is that he loathes the London mob—not because they wish him ill, but because they wish him well; not because they are baying for his blood, but because they can smell it).

A remarkable feature of the book is that although on the surface it seems to be a straightforward and seamless narrative it is no such thing. It is in fact a series of smoothly linked short stories. Not every chapter comprises a self-contained tale but certainly 'The Faithful Commons', 'The Outrage at the *Megaphone*', 'The Messenger of the Four' and even the 'inquest' chapter at the end have a beginning, a middle and a natural conclusion, and each is so constructed that either a problem is devised and then solved, or a shock or twist is contained in the climax. It was a style of storytelling—a series of minor mysteries solved in sequence throughout the book while the major mystery was only revealed at the end—that was to be refined over the years until it was recognisably the Wallacean method, to be cheerfully pinched by an entire generation of thriller writers.

Throughout the book there are some delightful touches. The vignettes of newspaper office life are amusingly and lovingly drawn; much sport is made of politicians. It's clear that Wallace had a great deal of fun in the writing: he chucks in Seneca's description of the Angry Man in the original Latin, old saws from Epictetus, and even foists on to one of his heroes the 'finest' translation of Lequetius' *Theologi Physiognomia Humana*. And whether Wallace ever had enough Latin to pronounce 'the cat sat on the mat' (very doubtful) doesn't matter a jot. What matters is that his enjoyment comes strikingly across to the reader.

But of course Wallace's main purpose was to thrill, and surely he does that. The Four, invincible as they may seem, do not have things all their own way. At times disaster looms; at times the game is very nearly up. Gradually the pace quickens, the tension is screwed up. Cleverly, indeed, cynically, Wallace persuades us to forget the essential amorality at the story's heart as the narrative builds to its final climax when it seems that all London throngs the Albert Embankment, eyes fixed on the farther shore, waiting and watching for a man to be killed.

THE FOUR JUST MEN

PROLOGUE

Thery's Trade

If you leave the Plaza del Mina, go down the narrow street, where, from ten till four, the big flag of the United States Consulate hangs lazily; through the square on which the Hotel de la France fronts, round by the Church of Our Lady, and along the clean, narrow thoroughfare that is the High Street of Cadiz, you will come to the Café of the Nations.

At five o'clock there will be few people in the broad, pillared saloon, and usually the little round tables that obstruct the sidewalk before its doors are untenanted.

In the late summer (in the year of the famine) four men sat about one table and talked business.

Leon Gonsalez was one, Poiccart was another, George Manfred was a notable third, and one, Thery, or Saimont, was the fourth. Of this quartet, only Thery requires no introduction to the student of contemporary history. In the Bureau of Public Affairs you will find his record. As Thery, alias Saimont, he is registered.

You may, if you are inquisitive, and have the necessary permission, inspect his photograph taken in eighteen positions—with his hands across his broad chest, full faced, with a three-days' growth of beard, profile, with—but why enumerate the whole eighteen?

There are also photographs of his ears—and very ugly, bat-shaped ears they are—and a long and comprehensive story of his life.

Signor Paolo Mantegazza, Director of the National Museum of Anthropology, Florence, has done Thery the honour of including him in his admirable work (see chapter

3

on 'Intellectual Value of a Face'); hence I say that to all students of criminology and physiognomy, Thery must need no introduction.

He sat at a little table, this man, obviously ill at ease, pinching his fat cheeks, smoothing his shaggy eyebrows, fingering the white scar on his unshaven chin, doing all the things that the lower classes do when they suddenly find themselves placed on terms of equality with their betters.

For although Gonsalez, with the light blue eyes and the restless hands, and Poiccart, heavy, saturnine, and suspicious, and George Manfred, with his grey-shot beard and single eyeglass, were less famous in the criminal world, each was a great man, as you shall learn.

Manfred laid down the *Heraldo di Madrid*, removed his eyeglass, rubbed it with a spotless handkerchief, and laughed quietly.

'These Russians are droll,' he commented.

Poiccart frowned and reached for the newspaper. 'Who is it—this time?'

'A governor of one of the Southern Provinces.'

'Killed?'

Manfred's moustache curled in scornful derision.

'Bah! Who ever killed a man with a bomb! Yes, yes; I know it has been done—but so clumsy, so primitive, so very much like undermining a city wall that it may fall and slay—amongst others—your enemy.'

Poiccart was reading the telegram deliberately and without haste, after his fashion.

'The Prince was severely injured and the would-be assassin lost an arm,' he read, and pursed his lips disapprovingly. The hands of Gonsalez, never still, opened and shut nervously, which was Leon's sign of perturbation.

'Our friend here'—Manfred jerked his head in the direction of Gonsalez and laughed—'our friend has a conscience and——'

'Only once,' interrupted Leon quickly, 'and not by my wish you remember, Manfred; you remember, Poiccart'—he did not address Thery—'I advised against it. You remember?' He seemed anxious to exculpate himself from the unspoken charge. 'It was a miserable little thing, and I was in Madrid,' he went on breathlessly, 'and they came to me, some men from a factory at Barcelona. They said what they were going to do, and I was horror-stricken at their ignorance of the elements of the laws of chemistry. I wrote down the ingredients and the proportions, and begged them, yes, almost on my knees, to use some other method. "My children," I said, "you are playing with something that even chemists are afraid to handle. If the owner of the factory is a bad man, by all means exterminate him, shoot him, wait on him after he has dined and is slow and dull, and present a petition with the right hand and—with the left hand—so!" '

Leon twisted his knuckles down and struck forward and upward at an imaginary oppressor. 'But they would listen to nothing I had to say.'

Manfred stirred the glass of creamy liquid that stood at his elbow and nodded his head with an amused twinkle in his grey eyes.

'I remember—several people died, and the principal witness at the trial of the expert in explosives was the man for whom the bomb was intended.'

Thery cleared his throat as if to speak, and the three looked at him curiously. There was some resentment in Thery's voice.

'I do not profess to be a great man like you, señors. Half the time I don't understand what you are talking about—you speak of governments and kings and constitutions and causes. If a man does *me* an injury I smash his head'—he hesitated—'I do not know how to say it . . . but I mean . . . well, you kill people without hating them, men who have not hurt you. Now, that is not my way . . .' He hesitated again, tried to collect his thoughts, looked intently at the middle of the roadway, shook his head, and relapsed into silence.

The others looked at him, then at one another, and each man smiled. Manfred took a bulky case from his pocket, extracted an untidy cigarette, re-rolled it deftly and struck a government match on the sole of his boot.

'Your-way-my-dear-Thery'—he puffed—'is a fool's way. You kill for benefit; we kill for justice, which lifts us out of the ruck of professional slayers. When we see an unjust man oppressing his fellows; when we see an evil thing done against the good God'—Thery crossed himself—'and against man— and know that by the laws of man this evildoer may escape punishment—we punish.'

'Listen,' interrupted the taciturn Poiccart: 'once there was a girl, young and beautiful, up there'—he waved his hand northward with unerring instinct—'and a priest—a priest, you understand—and the parents winked at it because it is often done . . . but the girl was filled with loathing and shame, and would not go a second time, so he trapped her and kept her in a house, and then when the bloom was off turned her out, and I found her. She was nothing to me, but I said, "Here is a wrong that the law cannot adequately right." So one night I called on the priest with my hat over my eyes and said that I wanted him to come to a dying traveller. He would not have come then, but I told him that the dying man was rich and was a great person. He mounted the horse I had brought, and we rode to a little house on the mountain . . . I locked the door and he turned round—so! Trapped, and he knew it. "What are you going to do?" he said with a gasping noise. "I am going to kill you, señor," I said, and he believed me. I told him the story of the girl. . . . He screamed when I moved towards him, but he might as well have saved his breath. "Let me see a priest," he begged; and I handed him—a mirror.'

Poiccart stopped to sip his coffee.

6

'They found him on the road next day without a mark to show how he died,' he said simply.

'How?' Thery bent forward eagerly, but Poiccart permitted himself to smile grimly, and made no response.

Thery bent his brows and looked suspiciously from one to the other.

'If you kill as you say you can, why have you sent for me? I was happy in Jerez working at the wine factory . . . there is a girl there . . . they call her Juan Samarez.' He mopped his forehead and looked quickly from one to the other. 'When I received your message I thought I should like to kill you—whoever you were—you understand I am happy . . . and there is the girl—and the old life I had forgotten——'

Manfred arrested the incoherent protests.

'Listen,' said he imperiously; 'it is not for you to inquire the wherefore and the why; we know who you are and what you are; we know more of you even than the police know, for we could send you to the garotte.'

Poiccart nodded his head in affirmation, and Gonsalez looked at Thery curiously, like the student of human nature that he was.

'We want a fourth man,' went on Manfred, 'for something we wish to do; we would have wished to have had one animated by no other desire than to see justice done. Failing that, we must have a criminal, a murderer if you like.'

Thery opened and shut his mouth as if about to speak.

'One whom we can at a word send to his death if he fails us; you are the man; you will run no risk; you will be well rewarded; you may not be asked to slay. Listen,' went on Manfred, seeing that Thery had opened his mouth to speak. 'Do you know England? I see that you do not. You know Gibraltar? Well, this is the same people. It is a country up there'—Manfred's expressive hands waved north—'a curious, dull country, with curious, dull people. There is a man, a member of the Government, and there are men whom the Government have never heard of. You remember one Garcia, Manuel Garcia, leader in the Carlist movement; he is in England; it is the only country where he is safe; from England he directs the movement here, the great movement. You know of what I speak?'

Thery nodded.

'This year as well as last there has been a famine, men have been dying about the church doors, starving in the public squares; they have watched corrupt Government succeed corrupt Government; they have seen millions flow from the public treasury into the pockets of politicians. This year something will happen; the old régime must go. The Government know this; they know where the danger lies, they know their salvation can only come if Garcia is delivered into their hands before the organisation for revolt is complete. But Garcia is safe for the present and would be safe for all time were it not for a member of the English Government, who is about to introduce and pass into law a Bill. When that is passed, Garcia is as good as dead. You must help us to prevent that from ever becoming law; that is why we have sent for you.'

Thery looked bewildered. 'But how?' he stammered.

Manfred drew a paper from his pocket and handed it to Thery. 'This, I think,' he said, speaking deliberately, 'is an exact copy of the police description of yourself.' Thery nodded. Manfred leant over and, pointing to a word that occurred half way down the sheet, 'Is that your trade?' he asked.

Thery looked puzzled. 'Yes,' he replied.

'Do you really know anything about that trade?' asked Manfred earnestly; and the other two men leant forward to catch the reply.

'I know,' said Thery slowly, 'everything there is to be known: had it not been for a—mistake I might have earned great money.'

8

Manfred heaved a sigh of relief and nodded to his two companions.

'Then,' said he briskly, 'the English Minister is a dead man.'

1

A Newspaper Story

On the fourteenth day of August, 19—, a tiny paragraph appeared at the foot of an unimportant page in London's most sober journal to the effect that the Secretary of State for Foreign Affairs had been much annoyed by the receipt of a number of threatening letters, and was prepared to pay a reward of fifty pounds to any person who would give such information as would lead to the apprehension and conviction of the person or persons, etc. The few people who read London's most sober journal thought, in their ponderous Athenæum Club way, that it was a remarkable thing that a Minister of State should be annoyed at anything; more remarkable that he should advertise his annoyance, and most remarkable of all that he could imagine for one minute that the offer of a reward would put a stop to the annoyance.

News editors of less sober but larger circulated newspapers, wearily scanning the dull columns of *Old Sobriety*, read the paragraph with a newly acquired interest.

'Hullo, what's this?' asked Smiles of the *Comet*, and cut out the paragraph with huge shears, pasted it upon a sheet of copy-paper and headed it:

Who is Sir Philip's Correspondent?

As an afterthought—the *Comet* being in Opposition—he prefixed an introductory paragraph, humorously suggesting that the letters were from an intelligent electorate grown tired of the shilly-shallying methods of the Government.

The news editor of the *Evening World*—a white-haired gentleman of deliberate movement—read the paragraph twice, cut it out carefully, read it again and, placing it under a paperweight, very soon forgot all about it.

The news editor of the *Megaphone*, which is a very bright newspaper indeed, cut the paragraph as he read it, rang a bell, called a reporter, all in a breath, so to speak, and issued a few terse instructions.

'Go down to Portland Place, try to see Sir Philip Ramon, secure the story of that paragraph—why he is threatened, what he is threatened with; get a copy of one of the letters if you can. If you cannot see Ramon, get hold of a secretary.'

And the obedient reporter went forth.

He returned in an hour in that state of mysterious agitation peculiar to the reporter who has got a 'beat'. The news editor duly reported to the Editor-in-Chief, and that great man said, 'That's very good, that's very good indeed'—which was praise of the highest order.

What was 'very good indeed' about the reporter's story may be gathered from the half-column that appeared in the *Megaphone* on the following day:

CABINET MINISTER IN DANGER
THREATS TO MURDER THE FOREIGN SECRETARY
'THE FOUR JUST MEN'
PLOT TO ARREST THE PASSAGE OF THE
ALIENS EXTRADITION BILL
EXTRAORDINARY REVELATIONS

Considerable comment was excited by the appearance in the news columns of yesterday's *National Journal* of the following paragraph:

The Secretary of State for Foreign Affairs (Sir Philip Ramon) has during the past few weeks been the recipient of threatening letters, all apparently emanating from one source and written by one person. These letters are of such a character that they cannot be ignored by his Majesty's Secretary of State for Foreign Affairs, who hereby offers a reward of Fifty pounds (£50) to any person or persons, other than the actual writer, who will lay such information as will lead to the apprehension and conviction of the author of these anonymous letters.

So unusual was such an announcement, remembering that anonymous and threatening letters are usually to be found daily in the letter-bags of every statesman and diplomat, that the *Daily Megaphone* immediately instituted inquiries as to the cause for this unusual departure.

A representative of this newspaper called at the residence of Sir Philip Ramon, who very courteously consented to be seen.

'It is quite an unusual step to take,' said the great Foreign Secretary, in answer to our representative's question, 'but it has been taken with the full concurrence of my colleagues of the Cabinet. We have reasons to believe there is something behind the threats, and I might say that the matter has been in the hands of the police for some weeks past.

'Here is one of the letters,' and Sir Philip produced a sheet of foreign notepaper from a portfolio, and was good enough to allow our representative to make a copy.

It was undated, and beyond the fact that the handwriting was of the flourishing effeminate variety that is characteristic of the Latin races, it was written in good English.

It ran:

> *Your Excellency,—*
> *The Bill that you are about to pass into law is an unjust one. . . . It is calculated to hand over to a corrupt and vengeful Government men who now in England find an asylum from the persecutions of despots and tyrants. We know that in England opinion is divided upon the merits of your Bill, and that upon your strength, and your strength alone, depends the passing into law of the Aliens Political Offences Bill.*

13

Therefore it grieves us to warn you that unless your Government withdraws this Bill, it will be necessary to remove you, and not alone you, but any other person who undertakes to carry into law this unjust measure.

(Signed) FOUR JUST MEN.

'The Bill referred to,' Sir Philip resumed, 'is of course the Aliens Extradition (Political Offences) Bill, which, had it not been for the tactics of the Opposition, might have passed quietly into law last session.'

Sir Philip went on to explain that the Bill was called into being by the insecurity of the succession in Spain.

'It is imperative that neither England nor any other country should harbour propagandists who, from the security of these, or other shores, should set Europe ablaze. Coincident with the passage of this measure similar Acts or proclamations have been made in every country in Europe. In fact, they are all in existence, having been arranged to come into law simultaneously with ours, last session.'

'Why do you attach importance to these letters?' asked the *Daily Megaphone* representative.

'Because we are assured, both by our own police and the continental police, that the writers are men who are in deadly earnest. The "FOUR JUST MEN", as they sign themselves, are known collectively in almost every country under the sun. Who they are individually we should all very much like to know. Rightly or wrongly, they consider that justice as meted out here on earth is inadequate, and have set themselves about correcting the law. They were the people who assassinated General Trelovitch, the leader of the Servian Regicides: they hanged the French Army Contractor, Conrad, in the Place de la Concorde—with a hundred policemen within call. They shot Hermon le Blois, the poet-philosopher, in his study for corrupting the youth of the world with his reasoning.'

14

The Foreign Secretary then handed to our representative a list of crimes committed by this extraordinary quartet.

Our readers will recollect the circumstance of each murder, and it will be remembered that until today—so closely have the police of the various nationalities kept the secret of the Four Men—no one crime has been connected with the other; and certainly none of the circumstances which, had they been published, would have assuredly revealed the existence of this band, have been given to the public before today.

The *Daily Megaphone* is able to publish a full list of sixteen murders committed by the four men.

'Two years ago, after the shooting of le Blois, by some hitch in their almost perfect arrangements, one of the four was recognised by a detective as having been seen leaving le Blois's house on the Avenue Kléber, and he was shadowed for three days, in the hope that the four might be captured together. In the end he discovered he was being watched, and made a bolt for liberty. He was driven to bay in a café in Bordeaux—they had followed him from Paris: and before he was killed he shot a sergeant de ville and two other policemen. He was photographed, and the print was circulated throughout Europe, but who he was or what he was, even what nationality he was, is a mystery to this day.'

'But the four are still in existence?'

Sir Philip shrugged his shoulders. 'They have either recruited another, or they are working shorthanded,' he said.

In conclusion the Foreign Secretary said:

'I am making this public through the Press, in order that the danger which threatens, not necessarily myself, but any public man who runs counter to the wishes of this sinister force, should be recognised. My second reason is that the public may in its knowledge assist those responsible for the maintenance of law and order in the execution of their office, and by their vigilance prevent the committal of further unlawful acts.'

Inquiries subsequently made at Scotland Yard elicited no further information on the subject beyond the fact that the Criminal Investigation Department was in communication with the chiefs of the continental police.

The following is a complete list of the murders committed by the Four Just Men, together with such particulars as the police have been able to secure regarding the cause for the crimes. We are indebted to the Foreign Office for permission to reproduce the list.

London, October 7, 1899.—Thomas Cutler, master tailor, found dead under suspicious circumstances. Coroner's jury returned a verdict of 'Wilful murder against some person or persons unknown'.

(Cause of murder ascertained by police: Cutler, who was a man of some substance, and whose real name was Bentvitch, was a sweater of a particularly offensive type. Three convictions under the Factory Act. Believed by the police there was a further and more intimate cause for the murder not unconnected with Cutler's treatment of women employees.)

Liege, February 28, 1900.—Jacques Ellerman, prefect: shot dead returning from the Opera House. Ellerman was a notorious evil liver, and upon investigating his affairs after his death it was found that he had embezzled nearly a quarter of a million francs of the public funds.

Seattle (Kentucky), October, 1900.—Judge Anderson. Found dead in his room, strangled. Anderson had thrice been tried for his life on charges of murder. He was the leader of the Anderson faction in the Anderson-Hara feud. Had killed in all seven of the Hara clan, was three times indicted and three times released on a verdict of Not Guilty. It will be remembered that on the last occasion, when charged with the treacherous murder of the Editor of the *Seattle Star*, he shook hands with the packed jury and congratulated them.

New York, October 30, 1900.—Patrick Welch, a notorious grafter and stealer of public moneys. Sometime City Treasurer; moving spirit in the infamous Street Paving Syndicate; exposed by the *New York Journal*. Welch was found hanging in a little wood on Long Island. Believed at the time to have been suicide.

Paris, March 4, 1901.—Madame Despard. Asphyxiated. This also was regarded as suicide till certain information came to hands of French police. Of Madame Despard nothing good can be said. She was a notorious 'dealer in souls'.

Paris, March 4, 1902 (exactly a year later).—Monsieur Gabriel Lanfin, Minister of Communication. Found shot in his brougham in the Bois de Boulogne. His coachman was arrested but eventually discharged. The man swore he heard no shot or cry from his master. It was raining at the time, and there were few pedestrians in the Bois.

(Here followed ten other cases, all on a par with those quoted above, including the cases of Trelovitch and le Blois.)

*   *   *

It was undoubtedly a great story.

The Editor-in-Chief, seated in his office, read it over again and said, 'Very good indeed.'

The reporter—whose name was Smith—read it over and grew pleasantly warm at the consequences of his achievement.

The Foreign Secretary read it in bed as he sipped his morning tea, and frowningly wondered if he had said too much.

The chief of the French police read it—translated and telegraphed—in *Le Temps*, and furiously cursed the talkative Englishman who was upsetting his plans.

In Madrid, at the Café de la Paix, in the Place of the Sun,

Manfred, cynical, smiling, and sarcastic, read extracts to three men—two pleasantly amused, the other heavy-jowled and pasty of face, with the fear of death in his eyes.

2

The Faithful Commons

Somebody—was it Mr Gladstone?—placed it on record that there is nothing quite so dangerous, quite so ferocious, quite so terrifying as a mad sheep. Similarly, as we know, there is no person quite so indiscreet, quite so foolishly talkative, quite so amazingly gauche, as the diplomat who for some reason or other has run off the rails.

There comes a moment to the man who has trained himself to guard his tongue in the Councils of Nations, who has been schooled to walk warily amongst pitfalls digged cunningly by friendly Powers, when the practice and precept of many years are forgotten, and he behaves humanly. Why this should be has never been discovered by ordinary people, although the psychological minority who can generally explain the mental processes of their fellows, have doubtless very adequate and convincing reasons for these acts of disbalancement.

Sir Philip Ramon was a man of peculiar temperament. I doubt whether anything in the wide world would have arrested his purpose once his mind had been made up. He was a man of strong character, a firm, square-jawed, big-mouthed man, with that shade of blue in his eyes that one looks for in peculiarly heartless criminals, and particularly famous generals. And yet Sir Philip Ramon feared, as few men imagined he feared, the consequence of the task he had set himself.

There are thousands of men who are physically heroes and morally poltroons, men who would laugh at death—and live in terror of personal embarrassments. Coroner's courts listen daily to the tale of such men's lives—and deaths.

The Foreign Secretary reversed these qualities. Good animal men would unhesitatingly describe the Minister as a coward, for he feared pain and he feared death.

'If this thing is worrying you so much,' the Premier said kindly—it was at the Cabinet Council two days following the publication of the *Megaphone*'s story—'why don't you drop the Bill? After all, there are matters of greater importance to occupy the time of the House, and we are getting near the end of the session.'

An approving murmur went round the table.

'We have every excuse for dropping it. There must be a horrible slaughtering of the innocents—Braithewaite's Unemployed Bill must go; and what the country will say to that, Heaven only knows.'

'No, no!' The Foreign Secretary brought his fist down on the table with a crash. 'It shall go through; of that I am determined. We are breaking faith with the Cortes, we are breaking faith with France, we are breaking faith with every country in the Union. I have promised the passage of this measure—and we must go through with it, even though there are a thousand "Just Men", and a thousand threats.'

The Premier shrugged his shoulders.

'Forgive me for saying so, Ramon,' said Bolton, the Solicitor, 'but I can't help feeling you were rather indiscreet to give particulars to the Press as you did. Yes, I know we were agreed that you should have a free hand to deal with the matter as you wished, but somehow I did not think you would have been quite so—what shall I say?—candid.'

'My discretion in the matter, Sir George, is not a subject that I care to discuss,' replied Ramon stiffly.

Later, as he walked across Palace Yard with the youthful-looking Chancellor, Mr Solicitor-General, smarting under the rebuff, said, *à propos* of nothing, 'Silly old ass'. And the youthful guardian of Britain's finances smiled.

'If the truth be told,' he said, 'Ramon is in a most awful funk. The story of the Four Just Men is in all the clubs, and a man I met at the Carlton at lunch has rather convinced me that there is really something to be feared. He was quite serious about it—he's just returned from South America and has seen some of the work done by these men.'

'What was that?'

'A president or something of one of these rotten little republics . . . about eight months ago—you'll see it in the list. . . . They hanged him . . . most extraordinary thing in the world. They took him out of bed in the middle of the night, gagged him, blindfolded him, carried him to the public jail, gained admission, and hanged him on the public gallows—and escaped!'

Mr Solicitor saw the difficulties of such proceedings, and was about to ask for further information when an undersecretary buttonholed the Chancellor and bore him off. 'Absurd,' muttered Mr Solicitor crossly.

There were cheers for the Secretary for Foreign Affairs as his brougham swept through the crowd that lined the approaches to the House. He was in no wise exalted, for popularity was not a possession he craved. He knew instinctively that the cheers were called forth by the public's appreciation of his peril; and the knowledge chilled and irritated him. He would have liked to think that the people scoffed at the existence of this mysterious four—it would have given him some peace of mind had he been able to think 'the people have rejected the idea'.

For although popularity or unpopularity was outside his scheme of essentials, yet he had an unswerving faith in the brute instincts of the mob. He was surrounded in the lobby of the House with a crowd of eager men of his party, some quizzical, some anxious, all clamouring for the latest information—all slightly in fear of the acid-tongued Minister.

'Look here, Sir Philip'—it was the stout, tactless member

for West Brondesbury—'what is all this we hear about threatenin' letters? Surely you're not goin' to take notice of things of that sort—why, I get two or three every day of my life.'

The Minister strode impatiently away from the group, but Tester—the member—caught his arm.

'Look here——' he began.

'Go to the devil,' said the Foreign Secretary plainly, and walked quickly to his room.

'Beastly temper that man's got, to be sure,' said the honourable member despairingly. 'Fact is, old Ramon's in a blue funk. The idea of making a song about threatenin' letters! Why, I get——'

A group of men in the members' smoke room discussed the question of the Just Four in a perfectly unoriginal way.

'It's too ridiculous for words,' said one oracularly. 'Here are four men, a mythical four, arrayed against all the forces and established agencies of the most civilised nation on earth.'

'Except Germany,' interrupted Scott, MP, wisely.

'Oh, leave Germany out of it for goodness' sake,' begged the first speaker tartly. 'I do wish, Scott, we could discuss a subject in which the superiority of German institutions could not be introduced.'

'Impossible,' said the cheerful Scott, flinging loose the reins of his hobby horse: 'remember that in steel and iron alone the production per head of the employee has increased 43 per cent., that her shipping——'

'Do you think Ramon will withdraw the Bill?' asked the senior member for Aldgate East, disentangling his attention from the babble of statistics.

'Ramon? Not he—he'd sooner die.'

'It's a most unusual circumstance,' said Aldgate East; and three boroughs, a London suburb, and a midland town nodded and 'thought it was'.

'In the old days, when old Bascoe was a young member'—

Aldgate East indicated an aged senator bent and white of beard and hair, who was walking painfully toward a seat—'in the old days——'

'Thought old Bascoe had paired?' remarked an irrelevant listener.

'In the old days,' continued the member for the East End, 'before the Fenian trouble——'

'——talk of civilisation,' went on the enthusiastic Scott. 'Rheinbaken said last month in the Lower House, "Germany had reached that point where——" '

'If I were Ramon,' resumed Aldgate East profoundly, 'I know exactly what I should do. I should go to the police and say "Look here——" '

A bell rang furiously and continuously, and the members went scampering along the corridor. 'Division—'vision.'

Clause Nine of the Medway Improvement Bill having been satisfactorily settled and the words, 'Or as may hereafter be determined" added by a triumphant majority of twenty-four, the faithful Commons returned to the interrupted discussion.

'What I say, and what I've always said about a man in the Cabinet,' maintained an important individual, 'is that he must, if he is a true statesman, drop all consideration for his own personal feelings.'

'Hear!' applauded somebody.

'His own personal feelings,' repeated the orator. 'He must put his duty to the state before all other—er—considerations. You remember what I said to Barrington the other night when we were talking out the Estimates? I said, "The right honourable gentleman has not, cannot have, allowed for the strong and almost unanimous desires of the great body of the electorate. The action of a Minister of the Crown must primarily be governed by the intelligent judgment of the great body of the electorate, whose fine feelings"—no— "whose higher instincts"—no—that wasn't it—at any rate I made it very clear what the duty of a Minister was,' concluded the oracle lamely.

'Now I——' commenced Aldgate East, when an attendant approached with a tray on which lay a greenish-grey envelope.

'Has any gentleman dropped this?' he inquired, and, picking up the letter, the member fumbled for his eyeglasses.

'To the Members of the House of Commons,' he read, and looked over his pince-nez at the circle of men about him.

'Company prospectus,' said the stout member for West Brondesbury, who had joined the party; 'I get hundreds. Only the other day——'

'Too thin for a prospectus,' said Aldgate East, weighing the letter in his hand.

'Patent medicine, then,' persisted the light of Brondesbury. 'I get one every morning—"Don't burn the candle at both ends", and all that sort of rot. Last week a feller sent me——'

'Open it,' someone suggested, and the member obeyed. He read a few lines and turned red.

'Well, I'm damned!' he gasped, and read aloud:

CITIZENS,

The Government is about to pass into law a measure which will place in the hands of the most evil Government of modern times men who are patriots and who are destined to be the saviours of their countries. We have informed the Minister in charge of this measure, the title of which appears in the margin, that unless he withdraws this Bill we will surely slay him.

We are loath to take this extreme step, knowing that otherwise he is an honest and brave gentleman, and it is with a desire to avoid fulfilling our promise that we ask the members of the Mother of Parliaments to use their every influence to force the withdrawal of this Bill.

24

*Were we common murderers or clumsy anarchists we
could with ease wreak a blind and indiscriminate ven-
geance on the members of this assembly, and in proof
thereof, and as an earnest that our threat is no idle one,
we beg you to search beneath the table near the recess in
this room. There you will find a machine sufficiently
charged to destroy the greater portion of this building.*

(Signed) FOUR JUST MEN

*Postscript.—We have not placed either detonator or
fuse in the machine, which may therefore be handled
with impunity.*

As the reading of the letter proceeded the faces of the
listeners grew pallid.

There was something very convincing about the tone of the
letter, and instinctively all eyes sought the table near the
recess.

Yes, there was something, a square black something, and
the crowd of legislators shrank back. For a moment they
stood spellbound—and then there was a mad rush for the
door

*　　*　　*

'Was it a hoax?' asked the Prime Minister anxiously, but
the hastily summoned expert from Scotland Yard shook his
head.

'Just as the letter described it,' he said gravely, 'even to the
absence of fuses.'

'Was it really——'

'Enough to wreck the House, sir,' was the reply.

The Premier, with a troubled face, paced the floor of his
private room.

He stopped once to look moodily through the window that
gave a view of a crowded terrace and a mass of excited
politicians gesticulating and evidently all speaking at once.

'Very, very serious—very, very serious,' he muttered. Then aloud, 'We said so much we might as well continue. Give the newspapers as full an account of this afternoon's happenings as they think necessary—give them the text of the letter.' He pushed a button and his secretary entered noiselessly.

'Write to the Commissioner telling him to offer a reward of a thousand pounds for the arrest of the man who left this thing and a free pardon and the reward to any accomplice.'

The Secretary withdrew and the Scotland Yard expert waited.

'Have your people found how the machine was introduced?'

'No, sir; the police have all been relieved and been subjected to separate interrogation. They remember seeing no stranger either entering or leaving the House.'

The Premier pursed his lips in thought.

'Thank you,' he said simply, and the expert withdrew.

On the terrace Aldgate East and the oratorical member divided honours.

'I must have been standing quite close to it,' said the latter impressively; ' 'pon my word it makes me go cold all over to think about it. You remember, Mellin? I was saying about the duty of the Ministry——'

'I asked the waiter,' said the member for Aldgate to an interested circle, 'when he brought the letter: "Where did you find it?" "On the floor, sir!" he said. "I thought it was a medicine advertisement; I wasn't going to open it, only somebody——" '

'It was me,' claimed the stout gentleman from Brondesbury proudly; 'you remember I was saying——'

'I knew it was somebody,' continued Aldgate East graciously. 'I opened it and read the first few lines. "Bless my soul", I said ——'

'You said, "Well, I'm damned," ' corrected Brondesbury.

'Well, I know it was something very much to the point,' admitted Aldgate East. 'I read it—and, you'll quite understand, I couldn't grasp its significance, so to speak. Well——'

*   *   *

The three stalls reserved at the Star Music Hall in Oxford Street were occupied one by one. At half past seven prompt came Manfred, dressed quietly; at eight came Poiccart, a fairly prosperous middle-aged gentleman; at half past eight came Gonsalez, asking in perfect English for a programme. He seated himself between the two others.

When pit and gallery were roaring themselves hoarse over a patriotic song, Manfred smilingly turned to Leon, and said:

'I saw it in the evening papers.'

Leon nodded quickly.

'There was nearly trouble,' he said quietly. 'As I went in somebody said, "I thought Bascoe had paired," and one of them almost came up to me and spoke.'

3

One Thousand Pounds Reward

To say that England was stirred to its depths—to quote more than one leading article on the subject—by the extraordinary occurrence in the House of Commons, would be stating the matter exactly.

The first intimation of the existence of the Four Just Men had been received with pardonable derision, particularly by those newspapers that were behindhand with the first news.

Only the *Daily Megaphone* had truly and earnestly recognised how real was the danger which threatened the Minister in charge of the obnoxious Act. Now, however, even the most scornful could not ignore the significance of the communication that had so mysteriously found its way into the very heart of Britain's most jealously guarded institution. The story of the Bomb Outrage filled the pages of every newspaper throughout the country, and the latest daring venture of the Four was placarded the length and breadth of the Isles.

Stories, mostly apocryphal, of the men who were responsible for the newest sensation made their appearance from day to day, and there was no other topic in the mouths of men wherever they met but the strange quartet who seemed to hold the lives of the mighty in the hollows of their hands.

Never since the days of the Fenian outrages had the mind of the public been so filled with apprehension as it was during the two days following the appearance in the Commons of the 'blank bomb', as one journal felicitously described it.

Perhaps in exactly the same kind of apprehension, since there was a general belief, which grew out of the trend of the letters, that the Four menaced none other than one man.

The first intimation of their intentions had excited widespread interest. But the fact that the threat had been launched from a small French town, and that in consequence the danger was very remote, had somehow robbed the threat of some of its force. Such was the vague reasoning of an ungeographical people that did not realise that Dax is no farther from London than Aberdeen.

But here was the Hidden Terror in the Metropolis itself. Why, argued London, with suspicious sidelong glances, every man we rub elbows with may be one of the Four, and we none the wiser.

Heavy, black-looking posters stared down from blank walls, and filled the breadth of every police noticeboard.

£1000 REWARD

WHEREAS, on August 18, at about 4.30 o'clock in the afternoon, an infernal machine was deposited in the Members' Smoke-Room by some person or persons unknown.

AND WHEREAS there is reason to believe that the person or persons implicated in the disposal of the aforesaid machine are members of an organised body of criminals known as The Four Just Men, against whom warrants have been issued on charges of wilful murder in London, Paris, New York, New Orleans, Seattle (USA), Barcelona, Tomsk, Belgrade, Christiania, Capetown and Caracas.

NOW, THEREFORE, the above reward will be paid by his Majesty's Government to any person or persons who shall lay such information as shall lead to the apprehension of any of or the whole of the persons styling themselves The Four Just Men and identical with the band before mentioned.

AND, FURTHERMORE, a free pardon and the

reward will be paid to any member of the band for
such information, providing the person laying such
information has neither committed nor has been an
accessory before or after the act of any of the following murders.

(*Signed*) RYDAY MONTGOMERY,

His Majesty's Secretary of State for Home
Affairs.

J. B. CALFORT, Commissioner of Police.

[Here followed a list of the sixteen crimes alleged
against the four men.]

GOD SAVE THE KING

All day long little knots of people gathered before the
broadsheets, digesting the magnificent offer.

It was an unusual hue and cry, differing from those with
which Londoners were best acquainted. For there was no
appended description of the men wanted; no portraits by
which they might be identified, no stereotyped 'when last
seen was wearing a dark blue serge suit, cloth cap, check tie',
on which the searcher might base his scrutiny of the passer-
by.

It was a search for four men whom no person had ever
consciously seen, a hunt for a will-o'-the-wisp, a groping in
the dark after indefinite shadows.

Detective Superintendent Falmouth, who was a very
plain-spoken man (he once brusquely explained to a Royal
Personage that he hadn't got eyes in the back of his head),
told the Assistant Commissioner exactly what he thought
about it.

'You can't catch men when you haven't got the slightest
idea who or what you're looking for. For the sake of argument, they might be women for all we know—they might be
chinamen or niggers; they might be tall or short; they might
—why, we don't even know their nationality! They've

30

committed crimes in almost every country in the world. They're not French because they killed a man in Paris, or Yankee because they strangled Judge Anderson.'

'The writing,' said the Commissioner, referring to a bunch of letters he held in his hand.

'Latin; but that may be a fake. And suppose it isn't? There's no difference between the handwriting of a Frenchman, Spaniard, Portuguese, Italian, South American, or Creole—and, as I say, it might be a fake, and probably is.'

'What have you done?' asked the Commissioner.

'We've pulled in all the suspicious characters we know. We've cleaned out Little Italy, combed Bloomsbury, been through Soho, and searched all the colonies. We raided a place at Nunhead last night—a lot of Armenians live down there, but——'

The detective's face bore a hopeless look.

'As likely as not,' he went on, 'we should find them at one of the swagger hotels—that's if they were fools enough to bunch together; but you may be sure they're living apart, and meeting at some unlikely spot once or twice a day.'

He paused, and tapped his fingers absently on the big desk at which he and his superior sat.

'We've had de Courville over,' he resumed. 'He saw the Soho crowd, and what is more important, saw his own man who lives amongst them—and it's none of them, I'll swear— or at least he swears, and I'm prepared to accept his word.'

The Commissioner shook his head pathetically.

'They're in an awful stew in Downing Street,' he said. 'They do not know exactly what is going to happen next.'

Mr Falmouth rose to his feet with a sigh and fingered the brim of his hat.

'Nice time ahead of us—I don't think,' he remarked paradoxically.

'What are the people thinking about it?' asked the Commissioner.

31

'You've seen the papers?'

Mr Commissioner's shrug was uncomplimentary to British journalism.

'The papers! Who in Heaven's name is going to take the slightest notice of what is in the papers!' he said petulantly.

'I am, for one,' replied the calm detective; 'newspapers are more often than not led by the public; and it seems to me the idea of running a newspaper in a nutshell is to write so that the public will say, "That's smart—it's what I've said all along." '

'But the public themselves—have you had an opportunity of gathering their idea?'

Superintendent Falmouth nodded.

'I was talking in the Park to a man only this evening—a master-man by the look of him, and presumably intelligent. "What's your idea of this Four Just Men business?" I asked. "It's very queer," he said: "do you think there's anything in it?"—and that,' concluded the disgusted police officer, 'is all the public thinks about it.'

But if there was sorrow at Scotland Yard, Fleet Street itself was all a-twitter with pleasurable excitement. Here was great news indeed: news that might be heralded across double columns, blared forth in headlines, shouted by placards, illustrated, diagramised, and illuminated by statistics.

'Is it the Mafia?' asked the *Comet* noisily, and went on to prove that it was.

The *Evening World*, with its editorial mind lingering lovingly in the 'sixties, mildly suggested a vendetta, and instanced 'The Corsican Brothers'.

The *Megaphone* stuck to the story of the Four Just Men, and printed pages of details concerning their nefarious acts. It disinterred from dusty files, continental and American, the full circumstances of each murder; it gave the portraits and careers of the men who were slain, and, whilst in no way palliating the offence of the Four, yet set forth justly and

32

dispassionately the lives of the victims, showing the sort of men they were.

It accepted warily the reams of contributions that flowed into the office; for a newspaper that has received the stigma 'yellow' exercises more caution than its more sober competitors. In newspaper-land a dull lie is seldom detected, but an interesting exaggeration drives an un-imaginative rival to hysterical denunciations.

And reams of Four Men anecdotes did flow in. For suddenly, as if by magic, every outside contributor, every literary gentleman who made a speciality of personal notes, every kind of man who wrote, discovered that he had known the Four intimately all his life.

'When I was in Italy . . .' wrote the author of *Come Again* (Hackworth Press, 6*s*.: 'slightly soiled', Farringdon Book Mart, 2*d*.) 'I remember I heard a curious story about these Men of Blood . . .'

Or——

'No spot in London is more likely to prove the hiding-place of the Four Villains than Tidal Basin,' wrote another gentleman, who stuck *Collins* in the north-east corner of his manuscript. 'Tidal Basin in the reign of Charles II was known as . . .'

'Who's Collins?' asked the super-chief of the *Megaphone* of his hard-worked editor.

'A liner,' described the editor wearily, thereby revealing that even the newer journalism had not driven the promiscuous contributor from his hard-fought field; 'he does police-courts, fires, inquests, and things. Lately he's taken to literature and writes Picturesque-Bits-of-Old-London and Famous Tombstones-of-Hornsey epics . . .'

Throughout the offices of the newspapers the same thing was happening. Every cable that arrived, every piece of information that reached the sub-editor's basket was coloured with the impending tragedy uppermost in men's

33

minds. Even the police-court reports contained some allu-
sion to the Four. It was the overnight drunk and disorderly's
justification for his indiscretion.

'The lad has always been honest,' said the peccant errand
boy's tearful mother; 'it's reading these horrible stories about
the Four Foreigners that's made him turn out like this'; and
the magistrate took a lenient view of the offence.

To all outward showing, Sir Philip Ramon, the man mostly
interested in the development of the plot, was the least
concerned.

He refused to be interviewed any further; he declined to
discuss the possibilities of assassination, even with the
Premier, and his answer to letters of appreciation that came
to him from all parts of the country was an announcement in
the *Morning Post* asking his correspondents to be good
enough to refrain from persecuting him with picture post-
cards, which found no other repository than his wastepaper
basket.

He had thought of adding an announcement of his intention of carrying the Bill through Parliament at whatever cost,
and was only deterred by the fear of theatricality.

To Falmouth, upon whom had naturally devolved the
duty of protecting the Foreign Secretary from harm, Sir
Philip was unusually gracious, and incidentally permitted
that astute officer to get a glimpse of the terror in which a
threatened man lives.

'Do you think there's any danger, Superintendent?' he
asked, not once but a score of times; and the officer, stout
defender of an infallible police force, was very reassuring.

'For,' as he argued to himself, 'what is the use of frighten-
ing a man who is half scared of death already? If nothing
happens, he will see I have spoken the truth, and if—if—well,
he won't be able to call me a liar.'

Sir Philip was a constant source of interest to the detective,
who must have shown his thoughts once or twice. For the

Foreign Secretary, who was a remarkably shrewd man, intercepting a curious glance of the police officer, said sharply, 'You wonder why I still go on with the Bill knowing the danger? Well, it will surprise you to learn that I do *not* know the danger, nor can I imagine it! I have never been conscious of physical pain in my life, and in spite of the fact that I have a weak heart, I have never had so much as a single ache. What death will be, what pangs or peace it may bring, I have no conception. I argue with Epictetus that the fear of death is by way of being an impertinent assumption of a knowledge of the hereafter, and that we have no reason to believe it is any worse condition than our present. I am not afraid to die—but I am afraid of dying.'

'Quite so, sir,' murmured the sympathetic but wholly uncomprehending detective, who had no mind for nice distinctions.

'But,' resumed the Minister—he was sitting in his study in Portland Place—'if I cannot imagine the exact process of dissolution, I can imagine and have experienced the result of breaking faith with the chancelleries, and I have certainly no intention of laying up a store of future embarrassments for fear of something that may after all be comparatively trifling.'

Which piece of reasoning will be sufficient to indicate what the Opposition of the hour was pleased to term 'the tortuous mind of the right honourable gentleman'.

And Superintendent Falmouth, listening with every indication of attention, yawned inwardly and wondered who Epictetus was.

'I have taken all possible precautions, sir,' said the detective in the pause that followed the recital of this creed. 'I hope you won't mind for a week or two being followed about by some of my men. I want you to allow two or three officers to remain in the house whilst you are here, and of course there will be quite a number on duty at the Foreign Office.'

Sir Philip expressed his approval, and later, when he and the detective drove down to the House in a closed brougham, he understood why cyclists rode before and on either side of the carriage, and why two cabs followed the brougham into Palace Yard.

At Notice Time, with a House sparsely filled, Sir Philip rose in his place and gave notice that he would move the second reading of the Aliens Extradition (Political Offences) Bill, on Tuesday week, or, to be exact, in ten days.

*   *   *

That evening Manfred met Gonsalez in North Tower Gardens and remarked on the fairy-like splendour of the Crystal Palace grounds by night.

A Guards' band was playing the overture to *Tannhäuser*, and the men talked music.

Then——

'What of Thery?' asked Manfred.

'Poiccart has him today; he is showing him the sights.' They both laughed.

'And you?' asked Gonsalez.

'I have had an interesting day; I met that delightfully naïve detective in Green Park, who asked me what I thought of ourselves!'

Gonsalez commented on the movement in G minor, and Manfred nodded his head, keeping time with the music.

'Are we prepared?' asked Leon quietly.

Manfred still nodded and softly whistled the number. He stopped with the final crash of the band, and joined in the applause that greeted the musicians.

'I have taken a place,' he said, clapping his hands. 'We had better come together.'

'Is everything there?'

Manfred looked at his companion with a twinkle in his eye.

'Almost everything.'

36

The band broke into the National Anthem, and the two men rose and uncovered.

The throng about the bandstand melted away in the gloom, and Manfred and his companion turned to go.

Thousands of fairy lamps gleamed in the grounds, and there was a strong smell of gas in the air.

'Not that way this time?' questioned, rather than asserted, Gonsalez.

'Most certainly not that way,' replied Manfred decidedly.

4

Preparations

When an advertisement appeared in the *Newspaper Proprietor* announcing that there was—

> FOR SALE: An old-established zinco-engraver's business with a splendid new plant and a stock of chemicals.

everybody in the printing world said 'That's Etherington's'. To the uninitiated a photo-engraver's is a place of buzzing saws, and lead shavings, and noisy lathes, and big bright arc lamps.

To the initiated a photo-engraver's is a place where works of art are reproduced by photography on zinc plates, and consequently used for printing purposes.

To the very knowing people of the printing world, Etherington's was the worst of its kind, producing the least presentable of pictures at a price slightly above the average.

Etherington's had been in the market (by order of the trustees) for three months, but partly owing to its remoteness from Fleet Street (it was in Carnaby Street), and partly to the dilapidated condition of the machinery (which shows that even an official receiver has no moral sense when he starts advertising), there had been no bids.

Manfred, who interviewed the trustee in Carey Street, learnt that the business could be either leased or purchased; that immediate possession in either circumstances was to be had; that there were premises at the top of the house which had served as a dwelling-place to generations of caretakers, and that a banker's reference was all that was necessary in the way of guarantee.

'Rather a crank,' said the trustee at a meeting of creditors, 'thinks that he is going to make a fortune turning out photo-gravures of Murillo at a price within reach of the inartistic. He tells me that he is forming a small company to carry on the business, and that so soon as it is formed he will buy the plant outright.'

And sure enough that very day Thomas Brown, merchant; Arthur W. Knight, gentleman; James Selkirk, artist; Andrew Cohen, financial agent; and James Leech, artist, wrote to the Registrar of Joint Stock Companies, asking to be formed into a company, limited by shares, with the object of carrying on business as photo-engravers, with which object they had severally subscribed for the shares set against their names.

(In parenthesis, Manfred was a great artist.)

And five days before the second reading of the Aliens Extradition Act, the company had entered into occupation of their new premises in preparation to starting business.

'Years ago, when I first came to London,' said Manfred, 'I learned the easiest way to conceal one's identity was to disguise oneself as a public enemy. There's a wealth of respectability behind the word "limited", and the pomp and circumstance of a company directorship diverts suspicion, even as it attracts attention.'

Gonsalez printed a neat notice to the effect that the Fine Arts Reproduction Syndicate would commence business on October 1, and a further neat label that 'no hands were wanted', and a further terse announcement that travellers and others could only be seen by appointment, and that all letters must be addressed to the Manager.

It was a plain-fronted shop, with a deep basement crowded with the dilapidated plant left by the liquidated engraver. The ground floor had been used as offices, and neglected furniture and grimy files predominated.

There were pigeonholes filled with old plates, pigeon-

holes filled with dusty invoices, pigeonholes in which all the
debris that is accumulated in an office by a clerk with salary
in arrear was deposited.

The first floor had been a workshop, the second had been a
store, and the third and most interesting floor of all was that
on which were the huge cameras and the powerful arc lamps
that were so necessary an adjunct to the business.

In the rear of the house on this floor were the three small
rooms that had served the purpose of the bygone caretaker.

In one of these, two days after the occupation, sat the four
men of Cadiz.

Autumn had come early in the year, a cold driving rain was
falling outside, and the fire that burnt in the Georgian grate
gave the chamber an air of comfort.

This room alone had been cleared of litter, the best furniture of the establishment had been introduced, and on the
ink-stained writing-table that filled the centre of the apartment stood the remains of a fairly luxurious lunch.

Gonsalez was reading a small red book, and it may be
remarked that he wore gold-rimmed spectacles; Poiccart was
sketching at a corner of the table, and Manfred was smoking
a long thin cigar and studying a manufacturing chemist's
price list. Thery (or as some prefer to call him Saimont) alone
did nothing, sitting a brooding heap before the fire, twid-
dling his fingers, and staring absently at the leaping little
flames in the gate.

Conversation was carried on spasmodically, as between
men whose minds were occupied by different thoughts.
Thery concentrated the attentions of the three by speaking to
the point. Turning from his study of the fire with a sudden
impulse he asked:

'How much longer am I to be kept here?'

Poiccart looked up from his drawing and remarked:

'That is the third time he has asked today.'

'Speak Spanish!' cried Thery passionately. 'I am tired of

40

this new language. I cannot understand it, any more than I can understand you.'

'You will wait till it is finished,' said Manfred, in the staccato patois of Andalusia; 'we have told you that.'

Thery growled and turned his face to the grate.

'I am tired of this life,' he said sullenly. 'I want to walk about without a guard—I want to go back to Jerez, where I was a free man. I am sorry I came away.'

'So am I,' said Manfred quietly; 'not very sorry though—I hope for your sake I shall not be.'

'Who are you?' burst forth Thery, after a momentary silence. 'What are you? Why do you wish to kill? Are you anarchists? What money do you make out of this? I want to know.'

Neither Poiccart nor Gonsalez nor Manfred showed any resentment at the peremptory demand of their recruit. Gonsalez's clean-shaven, sharp-pointed face twitched with pleasurable excitement, and his cold blue eyes narrowed.

'Perfect! perfect!' he murmured, watching the other man's face: 'pointed nose, small forehead and—*articulorum se ipsos torquentium sonus; gemitus, mugitusque parum explanatis*——'

The physiognomist might have continued Seneca's picture of the Angry Man, but Thery sprang to his feet and glowered at the three.

'Who are you?' he asked slowly. 'How do I know that you are not to get money for this? I want to know why you keep me a prisoner, why you will not let me see the newspapers, why you never allow me to walk alone in the street, or speak to somebody who knows my language? You are not from Spain, nor you, nor you—your Spanish is—yes, but you are not of the country I know. You want me to kill—but you will not say how——'

Manfred rose and laid his hand on the other's shoulder.

'Señor,' he said—and there was nothing but kindness in his eyes—'restrain your impatience, I beg of you. I again assure

41

you that we do not kill for gain. These two gentlemen whom you see have each fortunes exceeding six million pesetas, and I am even richer; we kill and we will kill because we are each sufferers through acts of injustice, for which the law gave us no remedy. If—if——' he hesitated, still keeping his grey eyes fixed unflinchingly on the Spaniard. Then he resumed gently: 'If we kill you it will be the first act of the kind.'

Thery was on his feet, white and snarling, with his back to the wall; a wolf at bay, looking from one to the other with fierce suspicion.

'Me—me!' he breathed, 'kill me?'

Neither of the three men moved save Manfred, who dropped his outstretched hand to his side.

'Yes, you.' He nodded as he spoke. 'It would be new work for us, for we have never slain except for justice—and to kill you would be an unjust thing.'

Poiccart looked at Thery pityingly.

'That is why we chose you,' said Poiccart, 'because there was always a fear of betrayal, and we thought—it had better be you.'

'Understand,' resumed Manfred calmly, 'that not a hair of your head will be harmed if you are faithful—that you will receive a reward that will enable you to live—remember the girl at Jerez.'

Thery sat down again with a shrug of indifference but his hands were trembling as he struck a match to light his cigarette.

'We will give you more freedom—you shall go out every day. In a few days we shall all return to Spain. They called you the silent man in the prison at Granada—we shall believe that you will remain so.'

After this the conversation became Greek to the Spaniard, for the men spoke in English.

'He gives very little trouble,' said Gonsalez. 'Now that we have dressed him like an Englishman, he does not attract attention. He doesn't like shaving every day; but it is necessary, and luckily he is fair. I do not allow him to speak in the street, and this tries his temper somewhat.'

Manfred turned the talk into a more serious channel.

'I shall send two more warnings, and one of those must be delivered in his very stronghold. He is a brave man.'

'What of Garcia?' asked Poiccart.

Manfred laughed.

'I saw him on Sunday night—a fine old man, fiery, and oratorical. I sat at the back of a little hall whilst he pleaded eloquently in French for the rights of man. He was a Jean-Jacques Rousseau, a Mirabeau, a broad-viewed Bright, and the audience was mostly composed of Cockney youths, who had come that they might boast they had stood in the temple of Anarchism.'

Poiccart tapped the table impatiently.

'Why is it, George, that an element of bathos comes into all these things?'

Manfred laughed.

'You remember Anderson? When we had gagged him and bound him to the chair, and had told him why he had to die—when there were only the pleading eyes of the condemned, and the half-dark room with a flickering lamp, and you and Leon and poor Clarice masked and silent, and I had just sentenced him to death—you remember how there crept into the room the scent of frying onions from the kitchen below.'

'I, too, remember,' said Leon, 'the case of the regicide.'

Poiccart made a motion of agreement.

'You mean the corsets,' he said, and the two nodded and laughed.

'There will always be bathos,' said Manfred; 'poor Garcia with a nation's destinies in his hand, an amusement for shop-girls—tragedy and the scent of onions—a rapier thrust and the whalebone of corsets—it is inseparable.'

43

And all the time Thery smoked cigarettes, looking into the fire with his head on his hands.

'Going back to this matter we have on our hands,' said Gonsalez. 'I suppose that there is nothing more to be done till—the day?'

'Nothing.'

'And after?'

'There are our fine art reproductions.'

'And after,' persisted Poiccart.

'There is a case in Holland, Hermannus van der Byl, to wit; but it will be simple, and there will be no necessity to warn.'

Poiccart's face was grave.

'I am glad you have suggested van der Byl, he should have been dealt with before—Hook of Holland or Flushing?'

'If we have time, the Hook by all means.'

'And Thery?'

'I will see to him,' said Gonsalez easily; 'we will go overland to Jerez—where the girl is,' he added laughingly.

The object of their discussion finished his tenth cigarette and sat up in his chair with a grunt.

'I forgot to tell you,' Leon went on, 'that today, when we were taking our exercise walk, Thery was considerably interested in the posters he saw everywhere, and was particularly curious to know why so many people were reading them. I had to find a lie on the spur of the minute, and I hate lying'—Gonsalez was perfectly sincere. 'I invented a story about racing or lotteries or something of the sort, and he was satisfied.'

Thery had caught his name in spite of its anglicised pronunciation, and looked inquiry.

'We will leave you to amuse our friend,' said Manfred rising. 'Poiccart and I have a few experiments to make.'

The two left the room, traversed the narrow passage, and paused before a small door at the end. A larger door on the

44

right, padlocked and barred, led to the studio. Drawing a small key from his pocket, Manfred opened the door, and, stepping into the room, switched on a light that shone dimly through a dust-covered bulb. There had been some attempt at restoring order from the chaos. Two shelves had been cleared of rubbish, and on these stood rows of bright little phials, each bearing a number. A rough table had been pushed against the wall beneath the shelves, and on the green baize with which the table was covered was a litter of graduated measures, test tubes, condensers, delicate scales, and two queer-shaped glass machines, not unlike gas generators.

Poiccart pulled a chair to the table, and gingerly lifted a metal cup that stood in a dish of water. Manfred, looking over his shoulder, remarked on the consistency of the liquid that half filled the vessel, and Poiccart bent his head, acknowledging the remark as though it were a compliment.

'Yes,' he said, satisfied, 'it is a complete success, the formula is quite right. Some day we may want to use this.'

He replaced the cup in its bath, and reaching beneath the table, produced from a pail a handful of ice-dust, with which he carefully surrounded the receptable.

'I regard that as the *multum in parvo* of explosives,' he said, and took down a small phial from the shelf, lifted the stopper with the crook of his little finger, and poured a few drops of a whitish liquid into the metal cup.

'That neutralises the elements,' said Poiccart, and gave a sigh of relief. 'I am not a nervous man, but the present is the first comfortable moment I have had for two days.'

'It makes an abominable smell,' said Manfred, with his handkerchief to his nose.

A thin smoke was rising from the cup.

'I never notice those things,' Poiccart replied, dipping a thin glass rod into the mess. He lifted the rod, and watched reddish drops dripping from the end.

'That's all right,' he said.

45

'And it is an explosive no more?' asked Manfred.

'It is as harmless as a cup of chocolate.'

Poiccart wiped the rod on a rag, replaced the phial, and turned to his companion.

'And now?' he asked.

Manfred made no answer, but unlocked an old-fashioned safe that stood in the corner of the room. From this he removed a box of polished wood. He opened the box and disclosed the contents.

'If Thery is the good workman he says he is, here is the bait that shall lure Sir Philip Ramon to his death,' he said.

Poiccart looked. 'Very ingenious,' was his only comment. Then—'Does Thery know, quite know, the stir it has created?'

Manfred closed the lid and replaced the box before he replied.

'Does Thery know that he is the fourth Just Man?' he asked; then slowly, 'I think not—and it is as well as he does not know; a thousand pounds is roughly thirty-three thousand pesetas, and there is the free pardon—and the girl at Jerez,' he added thoughtfully.

*　　*　　*

A brilliant idea came to Smith, the reporter, and he carried it to the chief.

'Not bad,' said the editor, which meant that the idea was really very good—'not bad at all.'

'It occurred to me,' said the gratified reporter, 'that one or two of the four might be foreigners who don't understand a word of English.'

'Quite so,' said the chief; 'thank you for the suggestion. I'll have it done tonight.'

Which dialogue accounts for the fact that the next morning the *Megaphone* appeared with the police notice in French, Italian, German—and Spanish.

46

5

The Outrage at the 'Megaphone'

The editor of the *Megaphone*, returning from dinner, met the super-chief on the stairs. The super-chief, boyish of face, withdrew his mind from the mental contemplation of a new project (Megaphone House is the home of new projects) and inquired after the Four Just Men.

'The excitement is keeping up,' replied the editor. 'People are talking of nothing else but the coming debate on the Extradition Bill, and the Government is taking every precaution against an attack upon Ramon.'

'What is the feeling?'

The editor shrugged his shoulders.

'Nobody really believes that anything will happen in spite of the bomb.'

The super-chief thought for a moment, and then quickly:

'What do *you* think?'

The editor laughed.

'I think the threat will never be fulfilled; for once the Four have struck against a snag. If they hadn't warned Ramon they might have done something, but forewarned——'

'We shall see,' said the super-chief, and went home.

The editor wondered, as he climbed the stairs, how much longer the Four would fill the contents bill of his newspaper, and rather hoped that they would make their attempt even though they met with a failure, which he regarded as inevitable.

His room was locked and in darkness, and he fumbled in his pocket for the key, found it, turned the lock, opened the door and entered.

'I wonder,' he mused, reaching out his hand and pressing down the switch of the light . . .

There was a blinding flash, a quick splutter of flame, and the room was in darkness again.

Startled, he retreated to the corridor and called for a light.

'Send for the electrician,' he roared; 'one of these damned fuses has gone!'

A lamp revealed the room to be filled with a pungent smoke; the electrician discovered that every globe had been carefully removed from its socket and placed on the table.

From one of the brackets suspended a curly length of thin wire which ended in a small black box, and it was from this that thick fumes were issuing.

'Open the windows,' directed the editor; and a bucket of water having been brought, the little box was dropped carefully into it.

Then it was that the editor discovered the letter—the greenish-grey letter that lay upon his desk. He took it up, turned it over, opened it, and noticed that the gum on the flap was still wet.

> *Honoured Sir* (ran the note), *when you turned on your light this evening you probably imagined for an instant that you were a victim of one of those 'outrages' to which you are fond of referring. We owe you an apology for any annoyance we may have caused you. The removal of your lamp and the substitution of a 'plug' connecting a small charge of magnesium powder is the cause of your discomfiture. We ask you to believe that it would have been as simple to have connected a charge of nitro-glycerine, and thus have made you your own executioner. We have arranged this as evidence of our inflexible intention to carry out our promise in respect of the Aliens Extradition Act. There is no power on earth that can save Sir Philip Ramon from destruc-*

tion, and we ask you, as the directing force of a great medium, to throw your weight into the scale in the cause of justice, to call upon your Government to withdraw an unjust measure, and save not only the lives of many inoffensive persons who have found an asylum in your country, but also the life of a Minister of the Crown whose only fault in our eyes is his zealousness in an unrighteous cause.

(Signed) THE FOUR JUST MEN

'Whew!' whistled the editor, wiping his forehead and eyeing the sodden box floating serenely at the top of the bucket.

'Anything wrong, sir?' asked the electrician daringly.

'Nothing,' was the sharp reply. 'Finish your work, refix these globes, and go.'

The electrician, ill-satisfied and curious, looked at the floating box and the broken length of wire.

'Curious-looking thing, sir,' he said. 'If you ask me——'

'I don't ask you anything; finish your work,' the great journalist interrupted.

'Beg pardon, I'm sure,' said the apologetic artisan.

Half an hour later the editor of the *Megaphone* sat discussing the situation with Welby.

Welby, who is the greatest foreign editor in London, grinned amiably and drawled his astonishment.

'I have always believed that these chaps meant business,' he said cheerfully, 'and what is more, I feel pretty certain that they will keep their promise. When I was in Genoa'—Welby got much of his information first-hand—'when I was in Genoa—or was it Sofia?—I met a man who told me about the Trelovitch affair. He was one of the men who assassinated the King of Servia, you remember. Well, one night he left his quarters to visit a theatre—the same night he was found dead in the public square with a sword thrust through his heart. There were two extraordinary things about it.' The foreign

49

editor ticked them off on his fingers. 'First, the General was a noted swordsman, and there was every evidence that he had not been killed in cold blood, but had been killed in a duel; the second was that he wore corsets, as many of these Germanised officers do, and one of his assailants had discovered this fact, probably by a sword thrust, and had made him discard them; at any rate when he was found this frippery was discovered close by his body.'

'Was it known at the time that it was the work of the Four?' asked the editor.

Welby shook his head.

'Even I had never heard of them before,' he said resentfully. Then asked, 'What have you done about your little scare?'

'I've seen the hall porters and the messengers, and every man on duty at the time, but the coming and the going of our mysterious friend—I don't suppose there was more than one—is unexplained. It really is a remarkable thing. Do you know, Welby, it gives me quite an uncanny feeling; the gum on the envelope was still wet; the letter must have been written on the premises and sealed down within a few seconds of my entering the room.'

'Were the windows open?'

'No; all three were shut and fastened, and it would have been impossible to enter the room that way.'

The detective who came to receive a report of the circumstances endorsed this opinion.

'The man who wrote this letter must have left your room not longer than a minute before you arrived,' he concluded, and took charge of the letter.

Being a young and enthusiastic detective, before finishing his investigations he made a most minute search of the room, turning up carpets, tapping walls, inspecting cupboards, and taking laborious and unnecessary measurements with a footrule.

'There are a lot of our chaps who sneer at detective stories,' he explained to the amused editor, 'but I have read almost everything that has been written by Gaboriau and Conan Doyle, and I believe in taking notice of little things. There wasn't any cigar ash or anything of that sort left behind, was there?' he asked wistfully.

'I'm afraid not,' said the editor gravely.

'Pity,' said the detective, and wrapping up the 'infernal machine' and its appurtenances, he took his departure.

Afterwards the editor informed Welby that the disciple of Holmes had spent half an hour with a magnifying glass examining the floor.

'He found half a sovereign that I lost weeks ago, so it's really an ill wind——'

All that evening nobody but Welby and the chief knew what had happened in the editor's room. There was some rumour in the sub-editor's department that a small accident had occurred in the sanctum.

'Chief busted a fuse in his room and got a devil of a fright,' said the man who attended to the Shipping List.

'Dear me,' said the weather expert, looking up from his chart, 'do you know something like that happened to me: the other night——'

The chief had directed a few firm words to the detective before his departure.

'Only you and myself know anything about this occurrence,' said the editor, 'so if it gets out I shall know it comes from Scotland Yard.'

'You may be sure nothing will come from us,' was the detective's reply: 'we've got into too much hot water already.'

'That's good,' said the editor, and 'that's good' sounded like a threat.

So that Welby and the chief kept the matter a secret till half an hour before the paper went to press.

This may seem to the layman an extraordinary circumstance, but experience has shown most men who control newspapers that news has an unlucky knack of leaking out before it appears in type.

Wicked compositors—and even compositors can be wicked—have been known to screw up copies of important exclusive news, and throw them out of a convenient window so that they have fallen close to a patient man standing in the street below and have been immediately hurried off to the office of a rival newspaper and sold for more than their weight in gold. Such cases have been known.

But at half past eleven the buzzing hive of Megaphone House began to hum, for then it was that the sub-editors learnt for the first time of the 'outrage'.

It was a great story—yet another *Megaphone* scoop, headlined half down the page with THE 'JUST FOUR' AGAIN—OUTRAGE AT THE OFFICE OF THE *Megaphone*—DEVILISH INGENUITY—*Another Threatening Letter—The Four Will Keep Their Promise—Remarkable Document—Will the Police save Sir Philip Ramon?*

'A very good story,' said the chief complacently, reading the proofs.

He was preparing to leave, and was speaking to Welby by the door.

'Not bad,' said the discriminating Welby. 'What I think—hullo!'

The last was addressed to a messenger who appeared with a stranger.

'Gentleman wants to speak to somebody, sir—bit excited, so I brought him up; he's a foreigner, and I can't understand him, so I brought him to you'—this to Welby.

'What do you want?' asked the chief in French.

The man shook his head, and said a few words in a strange tongue.

'Ah!' said Welby, 'Spanish—what do you wish?' he said in that language.

52

'Is this the office of that paper?' The man produced a grimy copy of the *Megaphone*.

'Yes.'

'Can I speak to the editor?'

The chief looked suspicious.

'I am the editor,' he said.

The man looked over his shoulder, then leant forward.

'I am one of The Four Just Men,' he said hesitatingly. Welby took a step towards him and scrutinised him closely.

'What is your name?' he asked quickly.

'Miguel Thery of Jerez,' replied the man.

*　　*　　*

It was half past ten when, returning from a concert, the cab that bore Poiccart and Manfred westward passed through Hanover Square and turned off to Oxford Street.

'You ask to see the editor,' Manfred was explaining; 'they take you up to the offices; you explain your business to somebody; they are very sorry, but they cannot help you; they are very polite, but not to the extent of seeing you off the premises, so, wandering about seeking your way out, you come to the editor's room, and, knowing that he is out, slip in, make your arrangements, walk out, locking the door after you if nobody is about, addressing a few farewell words to an imaginary occupant, if you are seen, and *voilà*!'

Poiccart bit the end of his cigar.

'Use for your envelope a gum that will not dry under an hour and you heighten the mystery,' he said quietly, and Manfred was amused.

'The envelope-just-fastened is an irresistible attraction to an English detective.'

The cab speeding along Oxford Street turned into Edgware Road, when Manfred put up his hand and pushed open the trap in the roof.

53

'We'll get down here,' he called, and the driver pulled up to the sidewalk.

'I thought you said Pembridge Gardens?' he remarked as Manfred paid him.

'So I did,' said Manfred; 'goodnight.'

They waited chatting on the edge of the pavement until the cab had disappeared from view, then turned back to the Marble Arch, crossed to Park Lane, walked down that plutocratic thoroughfare and round into Piccadilly. Near the Circus they found a restaurant with a long bar and many small alcoves, where men sat around marble tables, drinking, smoking, and talking. In one of these, alone, sat Gonsalez, smoking a long cigarette and wearing on his clean-shaven mobile face a look of meditative content.

Neither of the men evinced the slightest sign of surprise at meeting him—yet Manfred's heart missed a beat, and into the pallid cheeks of Poiccart crept two bright red spots.

They seated themselves, a waiter came and they gave their orders, and when he had gone Manfred asked in a low tone, 'Where is Thery?'

Leon gave the slightest shrug.

'Thery has made his escape,' he answered calmly.

For a minute neither man spoke, and Leon continued:

'This morning, before you left, you gave him a bundle of newspapers?'

Manfred nodded.

'They were English newspapers,' he said. 'Thery does not know a word of English. There were pictures in them—I gave them to amuse him.'

'You gave him, amongst others, the *Megaphone*?'

'Yes—ha!' Manfred remembered.

'The offer of a reward was in it—and the free pardon—printed in Spanish.'

Manfred was gazing into vacancy.

'I remember,' he said slowly. 'I read it afterwards.'

'It was very ingenious,' remarked Poiccart commendingly.

'I noticed he was rather excited, but I accounted for this by the fact that we had told him last night of the method we intended adopting for the removal of Ramon and the part he was to play.'

Leon changed the topic to allow the waiter to serve the refreshments that had been ordered.

'It is preposterous,' he went on without changing his key, 'that a horse on which so much money has been placed should not have been sent to England at least a month in advance.'

'The idea of a bad Channel-crossing leading to the scratching of the favourite of a big race is unheard of,' added Manfred severely.

The waiter left them.

'We went for a walk this afternoon,' resumed Leon, 'and were passing along Regent Street, he stopping every few seconds to look in the shops, when suddenly—we had been staring at the window of a photographer's—I missed him. There were hundreds of people in the street—but no Thery . . . I have been seeking him ever since.'

Leon sipped his drink and looked at his watch.

The other two men did nothing, said nothing.

A careful observer might have noticed that both Manfred's and Poiccart's hands strayed to the top button of their coats.

'Perhaps not so bad as that,' smiled Gonsalez.

Manfred broke the silence of the two.

'I take all blame,' he commenced, but Poiccart stopped him with a gesture.

'If there is any blame, I alone am blameless,' he said with a short laugh. 'No, George, it is too late to talk of blame. We underrated the cunning of m'sieur, the enterprise of the English newspapers and—and——'

'The girl at Jerez,' concluded Leon.

Five minutes passed in silence, each man thinking rapidly.

'I have a car not far from here,' said Leon at length. 'You

had told me you would be at this place by eleven o'clock; we have the naphtha launch at Burnham-on-Crouch—we could be in France by daybreak.'

Manfred looked at him. 'What do you think yourself?' he asked.

'I say stay and finish the work,' said Leon.

'And I,' said Poiccart quietly but decisively.

Manfred called the waiter.

'Have you the last editions of the evening papers?'

The waiter thought he could get them, and returned with two.

Manfred scanned the pages carefully, then threw them aside.

'Nothing in these,' he said. 'If Thery has gone to the police we must hide and use some other method to that agreed upon, or we could strike now. After all, Thery has told us all we want to know, but——'

'That would be unfair to Ramon.' Poiccart finished the sentence in such a tone as summarily ended that possibility. 'He has still two days, and must receive yet another, and last, warning.'

'Then we must find Thery.'

It was Manfred who spoke, and he rose, followed by Poiccart and Gonsalez.

'If Thery has not gone to the police—where would he go?'

The tone of Leon's question suggested the answer.

'To the office of the newspaper that published the Spanish advertisement,' was Manfred's reply, and instinctively the three men knew that this was the correct solution.

'Your motor-car will be useful,' said Manfred, and all three left the bar.

*　　*　　*

In the editor's room Thery faced the two journalists.

'Thery?' repeated Welby; 'I do not know that name.

Where do you come from? What is your address?'

'I come from Jerez in Andalusia, from the wine farm of Sienor.'

'Not that,' interrupted Welby; 'where do you come from now—what part of London?'

Thery raised his hands despairingly.

'How should I know? There are houses and streets and people—and it is in London, and I was to kill a man, a Minister, because he had made a wicked law—they did not tell me——'

'They—who?' asked the editor eagerly.

'The other three.'

'But their names?'

Thery shot a suspicious glance at his questioner.

'There is a reward,' he said sullenly, 'and a pardon. I want these before I tell——'

The editor stepped to his desk.

'If you are one of the Four you shall have your reward— you shall have some of it now.' He pressed a button and a messenger came to the door.

'Go to the composing room and tell the printer not to allow his men to leave until I give orders.'

Below, in the basement, the machines were thundering as they flung out the first numbers of the morning news.

'Now'—the editor turned to Thery, who had stood, uneasily shifting from foot to foot whilst the order was being given—'now, tell me all you know.'

Thery did not answer; his eyes were fixed on the floor.

'There is a reward and a pardon,' he muttered doggedly.

'Hasten!' cried Welby. 'You will receive your reward and the pardon also. Tell us, who are the Four Just Men? Who are the other three? Where are they to be found?'

'Here,' said a clear voice behind him; and he turned as a stranger, closing the door as he entered, stood facing the

57

three men—a stranger in evening dress, masked from brow to chin.

There was a revolver in the hand that hung at his side.

'I am one,' repeated the stranger calmly; 'there are two others waiting outside the building.'

'How did you get here—what do you want?' demanded the editor, and stretched his hand to an open drawer in his desk.

'Take your hand away'—and the thin barrel of the revolver rose with a jerk. 'How I came here your doorkeeper will explain, when he recovers consciousness. Why I am here is because I wish to save my life—not an unreasonable wish. If Thery speaks I may be a dead man—I am about to prevent him speaking. I have no quarrel with either of you gentlemen, but if you hinder me I shall kill you,' he said simply. He spoke all the while in English, and Thery, with wide-stretched eyes and distended nostrils, shrank back against the wall, breathing quickly.

'You,' said the masked man, turning to the terror-stricken informer and speaking in Spanish, 'would have betrayed your comrades—you would have thwarted a great purpose, therefore it is just that you should die.'

He raised the revolver to the level of Thery's breast, and Thery fell on his knees, mouthing the prayer he could not articulate.

'By God—no!' cried the editor, and sprang forward.

The revolver turned on him.

'Sir,' said the unknown—and his voice sank almost to a whisper—'for God's sake do not force me to kill you.'

'You shall not commit a cold-blooded murder,' cried the editor in a white heat of anger, and moved forward, but Welby held him back. 'What is the use?' said Welby in an undertone; 'he means it—we can do nothing.'

'You can do something,' said the stranger, and his revolver dropped to his side.

58

Before the editor could answer there was a knock at the door.

'Say you are busy'; and the revolver covered Thery, who was a whimpering, huddled heap by the wall.

'Go away,' shouted the editor, 'I am busy.'

'The printers are waiting,' said the voice of the messenger.

'Now,' asked the chief, as the footsteps of the boy died away; 'what can we do?'

'You can save this man's life.'

'How?'

'Give me your word of honour that you will allow us both to depart, and will neither raise an alarm nor leave this room for a quarter of an hour.'

The editor hesitated.

'How do I know that the murder you contemplate will not be committed as soon as you get clear?'

The other laughed under his mask.

'How do I know that as soon as I have left the room you will not raise an alarm?'

'I should have given my word, sir,' said the editor stiffly.

'And I mine,' was the quiet response. 'And my word has never been broken.'

In the editor's mind a struggle was going on; here in his hand was the greatest story of the century; another minute and he would have extracted from Thery the secret of the Four.

Even now a bold dash might save everything—and the printers were waiting . . . but the hand that held the revolver was the hand of a resolute man, and the chief yielded.

'I agree, but under protest,' he said. 'I warn you that your arrest and punishment is inevitable.'

'I regret,' said the masked man with a slight bow, 'that I cannot agree with you—nothing is inevitable save death. Come, Thery,' he said, speaking in Spanish. 'On my word as a Caballero I will not harm you.'

Thery hesitated, then slunk forward with his head bowed and his eyes fixed on the floor.

The masked man opened the door an inch, listened, and in the moment came the inspiration of the editor's life.

'Look here,' he said quickly, the man giving place to the journalist, 'when you get home will you write us an article about yourselves? You needn't give us any embarrassing particulars, you know—something about your aspirations, your *raison d'être.*'

'Sir,' said the masked man—and there was a note of admiration in his voice—'I recognise in you an artist. The article will be delivered tomorrow'; and opening the door the two men stepped into the darkened corridor.

6

The Clues

Blood-red placards, hoarse newsboys, overwhelming headlines, and column after column of leaded type told the world
next day how near the Four had been to capture. Men in the
train leant forward, their newspapers on their knees, and
explained what they would have done had they been in the
editor of the *Megaphone*'s position. People stopped talking
about wars and famines and droughts and street accidents
and parliaments and ordinary everyday murders and the
German Emperor, in order to concentrate their minds upon
the topic of the hour. Would the Four Just Men carry out
their promise and slay the Secretary for Foreign Affairs on
the morrow?

Nothing else was spoken about. Here was a murder threatened a month ago, and, unless something unforeseen
happened, to be committed tomorrow.

No wonder that the London Press devoted the greater
part of its space to discussing the coming of Thery and his
recapture.

'. . . It is not so easy to understand,' said the *Telegram*,
'why, having the miscreants in their hands, certain journalists connected with a sensational and halfpenny contemporary allowed them to go free to work their evil designs upon
a great statesman whose unparalleled . . . We say *if*, for
unfortunately in these days of cheap journalism every story
emanating from the sanctum sanctorum of sensation-loving
sheets is not to be accepted on its pretensions; so if, as it
stated, these desperadoes really did visit the office of a contemporary last night . . .'

At noonday Scotland Yard circulated broadcast a hastily printed sheet:

From which may be gathered that, acting on the information furnished by the editor and his assistant at two o'clock in the morning, the Direct Spanish Cable had been kept busy; important personages had been roused from their beds in Madrid, and the history of They as recorded in the Bureau had been reconstructed from pigeonhole records for the enlightenment of an energetic Commissioner of Police.

Sir Philip Ramon, sitting writing in his study at Portland Place, found a difficulty in keeping his mind upon the letter that lay before him.

It was a letter addressed to his agent at Branfell, the huge estate over which he, in the years he was out of office, played squire.

Neither wife nor chick nor child had Sir Philip. '. . . If by any chance these men succeed in carrying out their purpose I have made ample provision not only for yourself but for all who have rendered me faithful service,' he wrote—from which may be gathered the tenor of his letter.

During these past few weeks, Sir Philip's feelings towards the possible outcome of his action had undergone a change.

The irritation of a constant espionage, friendly on the one hand, menacing on the other, had engendered so bitter a feeling of resentment, that in this newer emotion all personal fear had been swallowed up. His mind was filled with one unswerving determination, to carry through the measure he had in hand, to thwart the Four Just Men, and to vindicate the integrity of a Minister of the Crown. 'It would be absurd,' he wrote in the course of an article entitled *Individuality in its Relation to the Public Service*, and which was published some months later in the *Quarterly Review*—'it would be monstrous to suppose that incidental criticism from a wholly unauthoritative source should affect or in any way influence a member of the Government in his conception of the legislation necessary for the millions of people entrusted to his care. He is the instrument, duly appointed, to put into tangible form the wishes and desires of those who naturally look to him not only to furnish means and methods for the betterment of their conditions, or the amelioration of irksome restrictions upon international commercial relations, but to find them protection from risks extraneous of purely commercial liabilities . . . in such a case a Minister of the Crown with a due appreciation of his responsibilities ceases to exist as a man and becomes merely an unhuman automaton.'

Sir Philip Ramon was a man with very few friends. He had none of the qualities that go to the making of a popular man. He was an honest man, a conscientious man, a strong man. He was the cold-blooded, cynical creature that a life devoid of love had left him. He had no enthusiasm—and inspired none. Satisfied that a certain procedure was less wrong than any other, he adopted it. Satisfied that a measure was for the immediate or ultimate good of his fellows, he carried that measure through to the bitter end. It may be said of him that

63

he had no ambitions—only aims. He was the most dangerous man in the Cabinet, which he dominated in his masterful way, for he knew not the meaning of the blessed word 'compromise'.

If he held views on any subject under the sun, those views were to be the views of his colleagues.

Four times in the short history of the administration had *Rumoured Resignation of a Cabinet Minister* filled the placards of the newspapers, and each time the Minister whose resignation was ultimately recorded was the man whose views had clashed with the Foreign Secretary. In small things, as in great, he had his way.

His official residence he absolutely refused to occupy, and No 44 Downing Street was converted into half office, half palace. Portland Place was his home, and from there he drove every morning, passing the Horse Guards clock as it finished the last stroke of ten.

A private telephone wire connected his study in Portland Place with the official residence, and but for this Sir Philip had cut himself adrift from the house in Downing Street, to occupy which had been the ambition of the great men of his party.

Now, however, with the approach of the day on which every effort would be taxed, the police insisted upon his taking up his quarters in Downing Street.

Here, they said, the task of protecting the Minister would be simplified. No 44 Downing Street they knew. The approaches could be better guarded, and, moreover, the drive—that dangerous drive!—between Portland Place and the Foreign Office would be obviated.

It took a considerable amount of pressure and pleading to induce Sir Philip to take even this step, and it was only when it was pointed out that the surveillance to which he was being subjected would not be so apparent to himself that he yielded.

'You don't like to find my men outside your door with your shaving water,' said Superintendent Falmouth bluntly. 'You objected to one of my men being in your bathroom when you went in the other morning, and you complained about a plain-clothes officer driving on your box—well, Sir Philip, in Downing Street I promise that you shan't even see them.'

This clinched the argument.

It was just before leaving Portland Place to take up his new quarters that he sat writing to his agent whilst the detective waited outside the door.

The telephone at Sir Philip's elbow buzzed—he hated bells—and the voice of his private secretary asked with some anxiety how long he would be.

'We have got sixty men on duty at 44,' said the secretary, zealous and young, 'and today and tomorrow we shall——' And Sir Philip listened with growing impatience to the recital.

'I wonder you have not got an iron safe to lock me in,' he said petulantly, and closed the conversation.

There was a knock at the door and Falmouth put his head inside.

'I don't want to hurry you, sir,' he said, 'but——'

So the Foreign Secretary drove off to Downing Street in something remarkably like a temper.

For he was not used to being hurried, or taken charge of, or ordered hither and thither. It irritated him further to see the now familiar cyclists on either side of the carriage, to recognise at every few yards an obvious policeman in mufti admiring the view from the sidewalk, and when he came to Downing Street and found it barred to all carriages but his own, and an enormous crowd of morbid sightseers gathered to cheer his ingress, he felt as he had never felt before in his life—humiliated.

He found his secretary waiting in his private office with the

65

rough draft of the speech that was to introduce the second reading of the Extradition Bill.

'We are pretty sure to meet with a great deal of opposition,' informed the secretary, 'but Mainland has sent out three-line whips, and expects to get a majority of thirty-six—at the very least.'

Ramon read over the notes and found them refreshing. They brought back the old feeling of security and importance. After all, he was a great Minister of State. Of course the threats were too absurd—the police were to blame for making so much fuss; and of course the Press—yes, that was it—a newspaper sensation.

There was something buoyant, something almost genial in his air, when he turned with a half smile to his secretary.

'Well, what about my unknown friends—what do the blackguards call themselves?—the Four Just Men?'

Even as he spoke he was acting a part; he had not forgotten their title, it was with him day and night.

The secretary hesitated; between his chief and himself the Four Just Men had been a tabooed subject.

'They—oh, we've heard nothing more than you have read,' he said lamely; 'we know now who Thery is, but we can't place his three companions.'

The Minister pursed his lips.

'They give me till tomorrow night to recant,' he said.

'You have heard from them again?'

'The briefest of notes,' said Sir Philip lightly.

'And otherwise?'

Sir Philip frowned. 'They will keep their promise,' he said shortly, for the 'otherwise' of his secretary had sent a coldness into his heart that he could not quite understand.

*   *   *

In the top room in the workshop at Carnaby Street, Thery, subdued, sullen, fearful, sat facing the three.

66

'I want you to quite understand,' said Manfred, 'that we bear you no ill-will for what you have done. I think, and Señor Poiccart thinks, that Señor Gonsalez did right to spare your life and bring you back to us.'

Thery dropped his eyes before the half-quizzical smile of the speaker.

'Tomorrow night you will do as you agreed to do—if the necessity still exists. Then you will go——' he paused.

'Where?' demanded Thery in sudden rage. 'Where in the name of Heaven? I have told them my name, they will know who I am—they will find that by writing to the police. Where am I to go?'

He sprang to his feet, glowering on the three men, his hands trembling with rage, his great frame shaking with the intensity of his anger.

'You betrayed yourself,' said Manfred quietly; 'that is your punishment. But we will find a place for you, a new Spain under other skies—and the girl at Jerez shall be there waiting for you.'

Thery looked from one to the other suspiciously. Were they laughing at him?

There was no smile on their faces; Gonsalez alone looked at him with keen, inquisitive eyes, as though he saw some hidden meaning in the speech.

'Will you swear that?' asked Thery hoarsely, 'will you swear that by the——'

'I promise that—if you wish it I will swear it,' said Manfred. 'And now,' he went on, his voice changing, 'you know what is expected of you tomorrow night—what you have to do?'

Thery nodded.

'There must be no hitch—no bungling; you and I and Poiccart and Gonsalez will kill this unjust man in a way that the world will never guess—such an execution as shall appal mankind. A swift death, a sure death, a death that will creep

67

through cracks, that will pass by the guards unnoticed. Why, there never has been such a thing done—such——' he stopped dead with flushed cheeks and kindling eyes, and met the gaze of his two companions. Poiccart impassive, sphinxlike, Leon interested and analytic. Manfred's face went a duller red.

'I am sorry,' he said almost humbly; 'for the moment I had forgotten the cause, and the end, in the strangeness of the means.'

He raised his hand deprecatingly.

'It is understandable,' said Poiccart gravely, and Leon pressed Manfred's arm.

The three stood in embarrassed silence for a moment, then Manfred laughed.

'To work!' he said, and led the way to the improvised laboratory.

Inside Thery took off his coat. Here was his province, and from being the cowed dependant he took charge of the party, directing them, instructing, commanding, until he had the men of whom, a few minutes before, he had stood in terror running from studio to laboratory, from floor to floor.

There was much to be done, much testing, much calculating, many little sums to be worked out on paper, for in the killing of Sir Philip Ramon all the resources of modern science were to be pressed into the service of the Four.

'I am going to survey the land,' said Manfred suddenly, and disappearing into the studio returned with a pair of step-ladders. These he straddled in the dark passage, and mounting quickly pushed up a trapdoor that led to the flat roof of the building.

He pulled himself up carefully, crawled along the leaden surface, and raising himself cautiously looked over the low parapet.

He was in the centre of a half mile circle of uneven roofs. Beyond the circumference of his horizon London loomed murkily through smoke and mist. Below was a busy street.

He took a hasty survey of the roof with its chimney stacks, its unornamental telegraph pole, its leaden floor and rusty guttering; then, through a pair of field-glasses, made a long, careful survey southward. He crawled slowly back to the trapdoor, raised it, and let himself down very gingerly till his feet touched the top of the ladder. Then he descended rapidly, closing the door after him.

'Well?' asked Thery with something of triumph in his voice.

'I see you have labelled it,' said Manfred.

'It is better so—since we shall work in the dark,' said Thery.

'Did you see then——?' began Poiccart.

Manfred nodded.

'Very indistinctly—one could just see the Houses of Parliament dimly, and Downing Street is a jumble of roofs.'

Thery had turned to the work that was engaging his attention. Whatever was his trade he was a deft workman. Somehow he felt that he must do his best for these men. He had been made forcibly aware of their superiority in the last days, he had now an ambition to assert his own skill, his individuality, and to earn commendation from these men who had made him feel his littleness.

Manfred and the others stood aside and watched him in silence. Leon, with a perplexed frown, kept his eyes fixed on the workman's face. For Leon Gonsalez, scientist, physiognomist (his translation of the *Theologi Physiognomia Humana* of Lequetius is regarded today as the finest), was endeavouring to reconcile the criminal with the artisan.

After a while Thery finished.

'All is now ready,' he said with a grin of satisfaction: 'let me find your Minister of State, give me a minute's speech with him, and the next minute he dies.'

His face, repulsive in repose, was now demoniacal. He was like some great bull from his own country made more terrible with the snuffle of blood in his nostrils.

In strange contrast were the faces of his employers. Not a muscle of either face stirred. There was neither exultation nor remorse in their expressions—only a curious something that creeps into the set face of the judge as he pronounces the dread sentence of the law. They saw that something, and it froze him to his very marrow.

He threw up his hands as if to ward them off.

'Stop! stop!' he shouted; 'don't look like that, in the name of God—don't, don't!' He covered his face with shaking hands.

'Like what, Thery?' asked Leon softly.

Thery shook his head.

'I cannot say—like the judge at Granada when he says—when he says, "Let the thing be done!" '

'If we look so,' said Manfred harshly, 'it is because we are judges—and not alone judges but executioners of our judgment.'

'I thought you would have been pleased,' whimpered Thery.

'You have done well,' said Manfred gravely.

'Bueno, bueno!' echoed the others.

'Pray God that we are successful,' added Manfred solemnly, and Thery stared at this strange man in amazement.

*   *   *

Superintendent Falmouth reported to the Commissioner that afternoon that all arrangements were now complete for the protection of the threatened Minister.

'I've filled up 44 Downing Street,' he said; 'there's practically a man in every room. I've got four of our best men on the roof, men in the basement, men in the kitchens.'

'What about the servants?' asked the Commissioner.

'Sir Philip has brought up his own people from the

country, and now there isn't a person in the house from the private secretary to the doorkeeper whose name and history I do not know from A to Z.'

The Commissioner breathed an anxious sigh.

'I shall be very glad when tomorrow is over,' he said. 'What are the final arrangements?'

'There has been no change, sir, since we fixed things up the morning Sir Philip came over. He remains at 44 all day tomorrow until half past eight, goes over to the House at nine to move the reading of the Bill, returns at eleven.'

'I have given orders for the traffic to be diverted along the Embankment between a quarter to nine and a quarter after, and the same at eleven,' said the Commissioner. 'Four closed carriages will drive from Downing Street to the House, Sir Philip will drive down in a car immediately afterwards.'

There was a rap at the door—the conversation took place in the Commissioner's office—and a police officer entered. He bore a card in his hand, which he laid upon the table.

'Señor Jose di Silva,' read the Commissioner, 'the Spanish Chief of Police,' he explained to the Superintendent. 'Show him in, please.'

Señor di Silva, a lithe little man, with a pronounced nose and a beard, greeted the Englishmen with the exaggerated politeness that is peculiar to Spanish official circles.

'I am sorry to bring you over,' said Mr Commissioner, after he had shaken hands with the visitor and had introduced him to Falmouth; 'we thought you might be able to help us in our search for Thery.'

'Luckily I was in Paris,' said the Spaniard; 'yes, I know Thery, and I am astounded to find him in such distinguished company. Do I know the Four?'—his shoulders went up to his ears—'Who does? I know of them—there was a case at Malaga, you know? . . . Thery is not a good criminal. I was astonished to learn that he had joined the band.'

'By the way,' said the chief, picking up a copy of the police

71

notice that lay on his desk, and running his eye over it, 'your people omitted to say—although it really isn't of very great importance—what is Thery's trade?'

The Spanish policeman knitted his brow.

'Thery's trade! Let me remember.' He thought for a moment. 'Thery's trade? I don't think I know; yet I have an idea that it is something to do with rubber. His first crime was stealing rubber; but if you want to know for certain——'

The Commissioner laughed.

'It really isn't at all important,' he said lightly.

7

The Messenger of the Four

There was yet another missive to be handed to the doomed Minister. In the last he had received there had occurred the sentence: *One more warning you shall receive, and so that we may be assured it shall not go astray, our next and last message shall be delivered into your hands by one of us in person.*

This passage afforded the police more comfort than had any episode since the beginning of the scare. They placed a curious faith in the honesty of the Four Men; they recognised that these were not ordinary criminals and that their pledge was inviolable. Indeed, had they thought otherwise the elaborate precautions that they were taking to ensure the safety of Sir Philip would not have been made. The honesty of the Four was their most terrible characteristic.

In this instance it served to raise a faint hope that the men who were setting at defiance the establishment of the law would overreach themselves. The letter conveying this message was the one to which Sir Philip had referred so airily in his conversation with his secretary. It had come by post, bearing the date mark, *Balham*, 12.15.

'The question is, shall we keep you absolutely surrounded, so that these men cannot by any possible chance carry out their threat?' asked Superintendent Falmouth in some perplexity, 'or shall we apparently relax our vigilance in order to lure one of the Four to his destruction?'

The question was directed to Sir Philip Ramon as he sat huddled up in the capacious depths of his office chair.

'You want to use me as a bait?' he asked sharply.

The detective expostulated.

'Not exactly that, sir; we want to give these men a chance——'

'I understand perfectly,' said the Minister, with some show of irritation.

The detective resumed:

'We know now how the infernal machine was smuggled into the House; on the day on which the outrage was committed an old member, Mr Bascoe, the member for North Torrington, was seen to enter the House.'

'Well?' asked Sir Philip in surprise.

'Mr Bascoe was never within a hundred miles of the House of Commons on that date,' said the detective quietly. 'We might never have found it out, for his name did not appear in the division list. We've been working quietly on that House of Commons affair ever since, and it was only a couple of days ago that we made the discovery.'

Sir Philip sprang from his chair and nervously paced the floor of his room.

'Then they are evidently well acquainted with the conditions of life in England,' he asserted rather than asked.

'Evidently; they've got the lie of the land, and that is one of the dangers of the situation.'

'But,' frowned the other, 'you have told me there were no dangers, no real dangers.'

'There is this danger, sir,' replied the detective, eyeing the Minister steadily, and dropping his voice as he spoke, 'men who are capable of making such disguise are really outside the ordinary run of criminals. I don't know what their game is, but whatever it is, they are playing it thoroughly. One of them is evidently an artist at that sort of thing, and he's the man I'm afraid of—today.'

Sir Philip's head tossed impatiently.

'I am tired of all this, tired of it'—and he thrashed the edge of his desk with an open palm—'detectives and disguises and masked murderers until the atmosphere is, for all the world, like that of a melodrama.'

'You must have patience for a day or two,' said the plain-spoken officer.

The Four Just Men were on the nerves of more people than the Foreign Minister.

'And we have not decided what is to be our plan for this evening,' he added.

'Do as you like,' said Sir Philip shortly, and then: 'Am I to be allowed to go to the House tonight?'

'No; that is not part of the programme,' replied the detective.

Sir Philip stood for a moment in thought.

'These arrangements; they are kept secret, I suppose?'

'Absolutely.'

'Who knows of them?'

'Yourself, the Commissioner, your secretary, and myself.'

'And no one else?'

'No one; there is no danger likely to arise from that source. If upon the secrecy of your movements your safety depended it would be plain sailing.'

'Have these arrangements been committed to writing?' asked Sir Philip.

'No, sir; nothing has been written; our plans have been settled upon and communicated verbally; even the Prime Minister does not know.'

Sir Philip breathed a sigh of relief.

'That is all to the good,' he said, as the detective rose to go.

'I must see the Commissioner. I shall be away for less than half an hour; in the meantime I suggest that you do not leave your room,' he said.

Sir Philip followed him out to the ante-room, in which sat Hamilton, the secretary.

'I have had an uncomfortable feeling,' said Falmouth, as one of his men approached with a long coat, which he proceeded to help the detective into, 'a sort of instinctive feeling this last day or two, that I have been watched and followed, so that I am using a car to convey me from place to place: they can't follow that, without attracting some notice.' He dipped his hand into the pocket and brought out a pair of motoring goggles. He laughed somewhat shamefacedly as he adjusted them. 'This is the only disguise I ever adopt, and I might say, Sir Philip,' he added with some regret, 'that this is the first time during my twenty-five years of service that I have ever played the fool like a stage detective.'

After Falmouth's departure the Foreign Minister returned to his desk.

He hated being alone: it frightened him. That there were two score detectives within call did not dispel the feeling of loneliness. The terror of the Four was ever with him, and this had so worked upon his nerves that the slightest noise irritated him. He played with the penholder that lay on the desk. He scribbled inconsequently on the blotting-pad before him, and was annoyed to find that the scribbling had taken the form of numbers of figure 4.

Was the Bill worth it? Was the sacrifice called for? Was the measure of such importance as to justify the risk? These things he asked himself again and again, and then immediately, What sacrifice? What risk?

'I am taking the consequence too much for granted,' he muttered, throwing aside the pen, and half turning from the writing-table. 'There is no certainty that they will keep their words; bah! it is impossible that they should——'

There was a knock at the door.

'Hullo, Superintendent,' said the Foreign Minister as the knocker entered. 'Back again already!'

The detective, vigorously brushing the dust from his moustache with a handkerchief, drew an official-looking blue envelope from his pocket.

'I thought I had better leave this in your care,' he said,

dropping his voice; 'it occurred to me just after I had left; accidents happen, you know.'

The Minister took the document.

'What is it?' he asked.

'It is something which would mean absolute disaster for me if by chance it was found in my possession,' said the detective, turning to go.

'What am I to do with it?'

'You would greatly oblige me by putting it in your desk until I return'; and the detective stepped into the ante-room, closed the door behind him and, acknowledging the salute of the plain-clothes officer who guarded the outer door, passed to the motor-car that awaited him.

Sir Philip looked at the envelope with a puzzled frown.

It bore the superscription *Confidential* and the address, *Department A, CID, Scotland Yard*.

'Some confidential report,' thought Sir Philip, and an angry doubt as to the possibility of it containing particulars of the police arrangements for his safety filled his mind. He had hit by accident upon the truth had he but known. The envelope contained those particulars.

He placed the letter in a drawer of his desk and drew some papers towards him.

They were copies of the Bill for the passage of which he was daring so much.

It was not a long document. The clauses were few in number, the objects, briefly described in the preamble, were tersely defined. There was no fear of this Bill failing to pass on the morrow. The Government's majority was assured. Men had been brought back to town, stragglers had been whipped in, prayers and threats alike had assisted in concentrating the rapidly dwindling strength of the administration on this one effort of legislation; and what the frantic entreaties of the Whips had failed to secure, curiosity had accomplished, for members of both parties were hurrying to town to be present at a scene which might perhaps be history, and, as many feared, tragedy.

As Sir Philip conned the paper he mechanically formed in his mind the line of attack—for, tragedy or no, the Bill struck at too many interests in the House to allow of its passage without a stormy debate. He was a master of dialectics, a brilliant casuist, a coiner of phrases that stuck and stung. There was nothing for him to fear in the debate. If only—— It hurt him to think of the Four Just Men. Not so much because they threatened his life—he had gone past that—but the mere thought that there had come a new factor into his calculations, a new and terrifying force, that could not be argued down or brushed aside with an acid jest, nor intrigued against, nor adjusted by any parliamentary method. He did not think of compromise. The possibility of making terms with his enemy never once entered his head.

'I'll go through with it!' he cried, not once but a score of times; 'I'll go through with it!' and now, as the moment grew nearer to hand, his determination to try conclusions with this new world-force grew stronger than ever.

The telephone at his elbow purred—he was sitting at his desk with his head on his hands—and he took the receiver. The voice of his house steward reminded him that he had arranged to give instructions for the closing of the house in Portland Place.

For two or three days, or until this terror had subsided, he intended his house should be empty. He would not risk the lives of his servants. If the Four intended to carry out their plan they would run no risks of failure, and if the method they employed were a bomb, then, to make assurance doubly sure, an explosion at Downing Street might well synchronise with an outrage at Portland Place.

He had finished his talk, and was replacing the receiver when a knock at the door heralded the entry of the detective.

He looked anxiously at the Minister.

'Nobody been, sir?' he asked.

Sir Philip smiled.

'If by that you mean have the Four delivered their ultimatum in person, I can comfort your mind—they have not.'

The detective's face was evidence of his relief.

'Thank Heaven!' he said fervently. 'I had an awful dread
that whilst I was away something would happen. But I have
news for you, sir.'

'Indeed!'

'Yes, sir, the Commissioner has received a long cable from
America. Since the two murders in that country one of
Pinkerton's men has been engaged in collecting data. For
years he has been piecing together the scrappy evidence he
has been able to secure, and this is his cablegram.' The
detective drew a paper from his pocket and, spreading it on
the desk, read:

> *Pinkerton, Chicago, to Commissioner of Police,*
> *Scotland Yard, London.*
>
> *Warn Ramon that the Four do not go outside their
> promise. If they have threatened to kill in a certain
> manner at a certain time they will be punctual. We have
> proof of this characteristic. After Anderson's death
> small memorandum book was discovered outside win-
> dow of room evidently dropped. Book was empty save
> for three pages, which were filled with neatly written
> memoranda headed 'Six methods of execution'. It was
> initialled 'C.' (third letter in alphabet). Warn Ramon
> against following: drinking coffee in any form, opening
> letters or parcels, using soap that has not been manufac-
> tured under eye of trustworthy agent, sitting in any room
> other than that occupied day and night by police officer.
> Examine his bedroom; see if there is any method by
> which heavy gases can be introduced. We are sending
> two men by 'Lucania' to watch.*

The detective finished reading. 'Watch' was not the last

79

word in the original message, as he knew. There had been an ominous postscript, *Afraid they will arrive too late*.

'Then you think——?' asked the statesman.

'That your danger lies in doing one of the things that Pinkerton warns us against,' replied the detective. 'There is no fear that the American police are talking idly. They have based their warning on some sure knowledge, and that is why I regard their cable as important.'

There was a sharp rap on the panel of the door, and without waiting for invitation the private secretary walked into the room, excitedly waving a newspaper.

'Look at this!' he cried, 'read this! The Four have admitted their failure.'

'What!' shouted the detective, reaching for the journal.

'What does this mean?' asked Sir Philip sharply.

'Only this, sir: these beggars, it appears, have actually written an article on their "mission".'

'In what newspaper?'

'The *Megaphone*. It seems when they recaptured Thery the editor asked the masked man to write him an article about himself, and they've done it; and it's here, and they've admitted defeat, and—and——'

The detective had seized the paper and broke in upon the incoherent secretary's speech.

'*The Creed of the Four Just Men*,' he read. 'Where is their confession of failure?'

'Half way down the column—I have marked the passage—here'; and the young man pointed with a trembling finger to a paragraph.

' "We leave nothing to chance," ' read the detective, ' "if the slightest hitch occurs, if the least detail of our plan miscarries, we acknowledge defeat. So assured are we that our presence on earth is necessary for the carrying out of a great plan, so certain are we that we are the indispensable instruments of a divine providence, that we dare not, for the sake of our very cause, accept unnecessary risks. It is essential therefore that the various preliminaries to every execution should be carried out to the full. As an example, it will be necessary for us to deliver our final warning to Sir Philip Ramon; and to add point to this warning, it is, by our code, essential that that should be handed to the Minister by one of us in person. All arrangements have been made to carry this portion of our programme into effect. But such are the extraordinary exigencies of our system that unless this warning can be handed to Sir Philip in accordance with our promise, and before eight o'clock this evening, our arrangements fall to the ground, and the execution we have planned must be forgone." '

The detective stopped reading, with disappointment visible on every line of his face.

'I thought, sir, by the way you were carrying on that you had discovered something new. I've read all this, a copy of the article was sent to the Yard as soon as it was received.'

The secretary thumped the desk impatiently.

'But don't you see!' he cried, 'don't you understand that there is no longer any need to guard Sir Philip, that there is no reason to use him as a bait, or, in fact, to do anything if we are to believe these men—look at the time——'

The detective's hand flew to his pocket; he drew out his watch, looked at the dial, and whistled.

'Half past eight, by God!' he muttered in astonishment, and the three stood in surprised silence.

Sir Philip broke the silence.

'Is it a ruse to take us off our guard?' he said hoarsely.

'I don't think so,' replied the detective slowly. 'I feel sure that it is not; nor shall I relax my watch—but I am a believer in the honesty of these men—I don't know why I should say this, for I have been dealing with criminals for the past twenty-five years, and never once have I put an ounce of faith in the word of the best of 'em, but somehow I can't disbelieve these men. If they have failed to deliver their message they will not trouble us again.'

Ramon paced his room with quick, nervous steps.

'I wish I could believe that,' he muttered; 'I wish I had your faith.'

A tap on the door panel.

'An urgent telegram for Sir Philip,' said a grey-haired attendant.

The Minister stretched out his hand, but the detective was before him.

'Remember Pinkerton's wire, sir,' he said, and ripped open the brown envelope.

> *Just received a telegram handed in at Charing Cross 7.52. Begins: We have delivered our last message to the Foreign Secretary, signed Four. Ends. Is this true? Editor, Megaphone.*

'What does this mean?' asked Falmouth in bewilderment when he had finished reading.

'It means, my dear Mr Falmouth,' replied Sir Philip testily, 'that your noble Four are liars and braggarts as well as murderers; and it means at the same time, I hope, an end to your ridiculous faith in their honesty.'

The detective made no answer, but his face was clouded and he bit his lips in perplexity.

'Nobody came after I left?' he asked.

'Nobody.'

'You have seen no person besides your secretary and myself?'

'Absolutely nobody has spoken to me, or approached within a dozen yards of me,' Ramon answered shortly.

Falmouth shook his head despairingly.

'Well—I—where are we?' he asked, speaking more to himself than to anybody in the room, and moved towards the door.

Then it was that Sir Philip remembered the package left in his charge.

'You had better take your precious documents,' he said, opening his drawer and throwing the package left in his charge on to the table.

The detective looked puzzled.

'What is this?' he asked, picking up the envelope.

'I'm afraid the shock of finding yourself deceived in your estimate of my persecutors has dazed you,' said Sir Philip, and added pointedly, 'I must ask the Commissioner to send an officer who has a better appreciation of the criminal mind, and a less childlike faith in the honour of murderers.'

'As to that, sir,' said Falmouth, unmoved by the outburst, 'you must do as you think best. I have discharged my duty to my own satisfaction; and I have no more critical taskmaster than myself. But what I am more anxious to hear is exactly what you mean by saying that I handed any papers into your care.'

The Foreign Secretary glanced across the table at the imperturbable police officer.

'I am referring, sir,' he said harshly, 'to the packet which you returned to leave in my charge.'

The detective stared.

'I—did—not—return,' he said in a strained voice. 'I have left no papers in your hands.' He picked up the package from the table, tore it open, and disclosed yet another envelope. As he caught sight of the grey-green cover he gave a sharp cry.

'This is the message of the Four,' said Falmouth.

The Foreign Secretary staggered back a pace, white to the lips.

'And the man who delivered it?' he gasped.

'Was one of the Four Just Men,' said the detective grimly. 'They have kept their promise.'

He took a quick step to the door, passed through into the

ante-room and beckoned the plain-clothes officer who stood on guard at the outer door.

'Do you remember my going out?' he asked.

'Yes, sir—both times.'

'Both times, eh!' said Falmouth bitterly, 'and how did I look the second time?'

His subordinate was bewildered at the form the question took.

'As usual, sir,' he stammered.

'How was I dressed?'

The constable considered.

'In your long dust-coat.'

'I wore my goggles, I suppose?'

'Yes, sir.'

'I thought so,' muttered Falmouth savagely, and raced down the broad marble stairs that led to the entrance-hall. There were four men on duty who saluted him as he approached.

'Do you remember my going out?' he asked of the sergeant in charge.

'Yes, sir—both times,' the officer replied.

'Damn your "both times"!' snapped Falmouth; 'how long had I been gone the first time before I returned?'

'Five minutes, sir,' was the astonished officer's reply.

'They just gave themselves time to do it,' muttered Falmouth, and then aloud, 'Did I return in my car?'

'Yes, sir.'

'Ah!'—hope sprang into the detective's breast—'did you notice the number?' he asked, almost fearful to hear the reply.

'Yes!'

The detective could have hugged the stolid officer.

'Good—what was it?'

'A17164.'

The detective made a rapid note of the number.

'Jackson,' he called, and one of the men in mufti stepped forward and saluted.

'Go to the Yard; find out the registered owner of this car. When you have found this go to the owner; ask him to explain his movements; if necessary, take him into custody.'

Falmouth retraced his steps to Sir Philip's study. He found the statesman still agitatedly walking up and down the room, the secretary nervously drumming his fingers on the table, and the letter still unopened.

'As I thought,' explained Falmouth, 'the man you saw was one of the Four impersonating me. He chose his time admirably: my own men were deceived. They managed to get a car exactly similar in build and colour to mine, and, watching their opportunity, they drove to Downing Street a few minutes after I had left. There is one last chance of our catching him—luckily the sergeant on duty noticed the number of the car, and we might be able to trace him through that—hullo.' An attendant stood at the door.

Would the Superintendent see Detective Jackson?

Falmouth found him waiting in the hall below.

'I beg your pardon, sir,' said Jackson, saluting, 'but is there not some mistake in this number?'

'Why?' asked the detective sharply.

'Because,' said the man. 'A17164 is the number of your own car.'

8

The Pocket-Book

The final warning was brief and to the point:

We allow you until tomorrow evening to reconsider your position in the matter of the Aliens Extradition Bill. If by six o'clock no announcement is made in the afternoon newspapers of your withdrawing this measure we shall have no other course to pursue but to fulfil our promise. You will die at eight in the evening. We append for your enlightenment a concise table of the secret police arrangements made for your safety tomorrow. Farewell.

(Signed) FOUR JUST MEN

Sir Philip read this over without a tremor. He read too the slip of paper on which were written, in the strange foreign hand, the details that the police had not dared to put into writing.

'There is a leakage somewhere,' he said, and the two anxious watchers saw that the face of their charge was grey and drawn.

'These details were known only to four,' said the detective quietly, 'and I'll stake my life that it was neither the Commissioner nor myself.'

'Nor I!' said the private secretary emphatically.

Sir Philip shrugged his shoulders with a weary laugh.

'What does it matter?—they know,' he exclaimed; 'by what uncanny method they learnt the secret I neither know nor care. The question is, can I be adequately protected tomorrow night at eight o'clock?'

Falmouth shut his teeth.

'Either you'll come out of it alive or, by the Lord, they'll kill two,' he said, and there was a gleam in his eye that spoke for his determination.

*   *   *

The news that yet another letter had reached the great statesman was on the streets at ten o'clock that night. It circulated through the clubs and theatres, and between the acts grave-faced men stood in the vestibules discussing Ramon's danger. The House of Commons was seething with excitement. In the hope that the Minister would come down, a strong House had gathered, but the members were disappointed, for it was evident soon after the dinner recess that Sir Philip had no intention of showing himself that night.

'Might I ask the right honourable the Prime Minister whether it is the intention of His Majesty's Government to proceed with the Aliens Extradition (Political Offences) Bill,' asked the Radical Member for West Deptford, 'and whether he has not considered, in view of the extraordinary conditions that this Bill has called into life, the advisability of postponing the introduction of this measure?'

The question was greeted with a chorus of 'hear-hears', and the Prime Minister rose slowly and turned an amused glance in the direction of the questioner.

'I know of no circumstance that is likely to prevent my right honourable friend, who is unfortunately not in his place tonight, from moving the second reading of the Bill to-morrow,' he said, and sat down.

'What the devil was he grinning at?' grumbled West Deptford to a neighbour.

'He's deuced uncomfortable, is JK,' said the other wisely, 'deuced uncomfortable; a man in the Cabinet was telling me today that old JK has been feeling deuced uncomfortable. "You mark my words," he said, "this Four Just Men

business is making the Premier deuced uncomfortable," '
and the hon. member subsided to allow West Deptford to
digest his neighbour's profundities.

'I've done my best to persuade Ramon to drop the Bill,' the
Premier was saying, 'but he is adamant, and the pitiable
thing is that he believes in his heart of hearts that these
fellows intend keeping faith.'

'It is monstrous,' said the Colonial Secretary hotly; 'it is
inconceivable that such a state of affairs can last. Why, it
strikes at the root of everything, it unbalances every adjust-
ment of civilisation.'

'It is a poetical idea,' said the phlegmatic Premier, 'and the
standpoint of the Four is quite a logical one. Think of the
enormous power for good or evil often vested in one man: a
capitalist controlling the markets of the world, a speculator
cornering cotton or wheat whilst mills stand idle and people
starve, tyrants and despots with the destinies of nations
between their thumb and finger—and then think of the four
men, known to none; vague, shadowy figures stalking tragic-
ally through the world, condemning and executing the
capitalist, the corner maker, the tyrant—evil forces all, and
all beyond reach of the law. We have said of these people,
such of us as are touched with mysticism, that God would
judge them. Here are men arrogating to themselves the
divine right of superior judgment. If we catch them they will
end their lives unpicturesquely, in a matter-of-fact, commonplace manner in a little shed in Pentonville Gaol, and the
world will never realise how great are the artists who perish.'

'But Ramon?'

The Premier smiled.

'Here, I think, these men have just overreached themselves. Had they been content to slay first and explain their
mission afterwards I have little doubt that Ramon would
have died. But they have warned and warned and exposed
their hand a dozen times over. I know nothing of the arrange-

ments that are being made by the police, but I should imagine that by tomorrow night it will be as difficult to get within a dozen yards of Ramon as it would be for a Siberian prisoner to dine with the Czar.'

'Is there no possibility of Ramon withdrawing the Bill?' asked the Colonies.

The Premier shook his head.

'Absolutely none,' he said.

The rising of a member of the Opposition front bench at that moment to move an amendment to a clause under discussion cut short the conversation.

The House rapidly emptied when it became generally known that Ramon did not intend appearing, and the members gathered in the smoking-room and lobby to speculate upon the matter which was uppermost in their minds.

In the vicinity of Palace Yard a great crowd had gathered, as in London crowds will gather, on the off-chance of catching a glimpse of the man whose name was in every mouth. Street vendors sold his portrait, frowsy men purveying the real life and adventures of the Four Just Men did a roaring trade, and itinerant street singers, introducing extemporised verses into their repertoire, declaimed the courage of that statesman bold, who dared for to resist the threats of coward alien and deadly anarchist.

There was praise in these poor lyrics for Sir Philip, who was trying to prevent the foreigner from taking the bread out of the mouths of honest working men.

The humour of which appealed greatly to Manfred, who, with Poiccart, had driven to the Westminster end of the Embankment; having dismissed their cab, they were walking to Whitehall.

'I think the verse about the "deadly foreign anarchist" taking the bread out of the mouth of the home-made variety is distinctly good,' chuckled Manfred.

Both men were in evening dress, and Poiccart wore in his

button-hole the silken button of a Chevalier of the Légion d'Honneur.

Manfred continued:

'I doubt whether London has had such a sensation since—when?'

Poiccart's grim smile caught the other's eye and he smiled in sympathy.

'Well?'

'I asked the same question of the maître d'hôtel,' he said slowly, like a man loath to share a joke; '*he* compared the agitation to the atrocious East-End murders.'

Manfred stopped dead and looked with horror on his companion.

'Great heavens!' he exclaimed in distress, 'it never occurred to me that we should be compared with—him!'

They resumed their walk.

'It is part of the eternal bathos,' said Poiccart serenely; 'even De Quincey taught the English nothing. The God of Justice has but one interpreter here, and he lives in a public-house in Lancashire, and is an expert and dexterous disciple of the lamented Marwood, whose system he has improved upon.'

They were traversing that portion of Whitehall from which Scotland Yard runs.

A man, slouching along with bent head and his hands thrust deep into the pockets of his tattered coat, gave them a swift sidelong glance, stopped when they had passed, and looked after them. Then he turned and quickened his shuffle on their trail. A press of people and a seeming ceaseless string of traffic at the corner of Cockspur Street brought Manfred and Poiccart to a standstill, waiting for an opportunity to cross the road. They were subjected to a little jostling as the knot of waiting people thickened, but eventually they crossed and walked towards St Martin's Lane.

The comparison which Poiccart had quoted still rankled with Manfred.

'There will be people at His Majesty's tonight,' he said, 'applauding Brutus as he asks, "What villain touched his body and not for justice?" You will not find a serious student of history, or any commonplace man of intelligence, for the matter of that, who, if you asked, Would it not have been God's blessing for the world if Bonaparte had been assassinated on his return from Egypt? would not answer without hesitation, Yes. But we—we are murderers!'

'They would not have erected a statue of Napoleon's assassin,' said Poiccart easily, 'any more than they have enshrined Felton, who slew a profligate and debauched Minister of Charles I. Posterity may do us justice,' he spoke half mockingly; 'for myself I am satisfied with the approval of my conscience.'

He threw away the cigar he was smoking, and put his hand to the inside pocket of his coat to find another. He withdrew his hand without the cigar and whistled a passing cab.

Manfred looked at him in surprise.

'What is the matter? I thought you said you would walk?'

Nevertheless he entered the hansom and Poiccart followed, giving his direction through the trap, 'Baker Street Station'.

The cab was rattling through Shaftesbury Avenue before Poiccart gave an explanation.

'I have been robbed,' he said, sinking his voice, 'my watch has gone, but that does not matter; the pocketbook with the notes I made for the guidance of Thery has gone—and that matters a great deal.'

'It may have been a common thief,' said Manfred: 'he took the watch.'

Poiccart was feeling his pockets rapidly.

'Nothing else has gone,' he said; 'it may have been as you say, a pickpocket, who will be content with the watch and will drop the notebook down the nearest drain; but it may be a police agent.'

'Was there anything in it to identify you?' asked Manfred, in a troubled tone.

'Nothing,' was the prompt reply; 'but unless the police are blind they would understand the calculations and the plans. It may not come to their hands at all, but if it does and the thief can recognise us we are in a fix.'

The cab drew up at the down station at Baker Street, and the two men alighted.

'I shall go east,' said Poiccart, 'we will meet in the morning. By that time I shall have learnt whether the book has reached Scotland Yard. Goodnight.'

And with no other farewell than this the two men parted.

*   *   *

If Billy Marks had not had a drop of drink he would have been perfectly satisfied with his night's work. Filled, however, with that false liquid confidence that leads so many good men astray, Billy thought it would be a sin to neglect the opportunities that the gods had shown him. The excitement engendered by the threats of the Four Just Men had brought all suburban London to Westminster, and on the Surrey side of the bridge Billy found hundreds of patient suburbanites waiting for conveyance to Streatham, Camberwell, Clapham, and Greenwich.

So, the night being comparatively young, Billy decided to work the trams.

He touched a purse from a stout old lady in black, a Waterbury watch from a gentleman in a top hat, a small hand mirror from a dainty bag, and decided to conclude his operations with the exploration of a superior young lady's pocket.

Billy's search was successful. A purse and a lace handkerchief rewarded him, and he made arrangements for a modest retirement. Then it was that a gentle voice breathed into his ear. 'Hullo, Billy!'

He knew the voice, and felt momentarily unwell.

'Hullo, Mister Howard,' he exclaimed with feigned joy; ' 'ow are you, sir? Fancy meetin' you!'

'Where are you going, Billy?' asked the welcome Mr Howard, taking Billy's arm affectionately.

' 'Ome,' said the virtuous Billy.

'Home it is,' said Mr Howard, leading the unwilling Billy from the crowd; 'home, sweet home, it is, Billy.' He called another young man, with whom he seemed to be acquainted: 'Go on that car, Porter, and see who has lost anything. If you can find anyone bring them along'; and the other young man obeyed.

'And now,' said Mr Howard, still holding Billy's arm affectionately, 'tell me how the world has been using you.'

'Look 'ere, Mr Howard,' said Billy earnestly, 'what's the game? where are you takin' me?'

'The game is the old game,' said Mr Howard sadly—'the same old game, Billy, and I'm taking you to the same old sweet spot.'

'You've made a mistake this time, guv'nor,' cried Bill fiercely, and there was a slight clink.

'Permit me, Billy,' said Mr Howard, stooping quickly and picking up the purse Billy had dropped.

At the police station the sergeant behind the charge desk pretended to be greatly overjoyed at Billy's arrival, and the gaoler, who put Billy into a steel-barred dock, and passed his hands through cunning pockets, greeted him as a friend.

'Gold watch, half a chain, gold, three purses, two handker-chiefs, and a red moroccer pocketbook,' reported the gaoler.

The sergeant nodded approvingly.

'Quite a good day's work, William,' he said.

'What shall I get this time?' inquired the prisoner, and Mr Howard, a plain-clothes officer engaged in filling in

93

particulars of the charge, opined nine moons.

'Go on!' exclaimed Mr Billy Marks in consternation.

'Fact,' said the sergeant; 'you're a rogue and a vagabond, Billy, you're a petty larcenist, and you're for the sessions this time—Number Eight.'

This latter was addressed to the gaoler, who bore Billy off to the cells protesting vigorously against a police force that could only tumble to poor blokes, and couldn't get a touch on sanguinary murderers like the Four Just Men.

'What do we pay rates and taxes for?' indignantly demanded Billy through the grating of his cell.

'Fat lot you'll ever pay, Billy,' said the gaoler, putting the double lock on the door.

In the charge office Mr Howard and the sergeant were examining the stolen property, and three owners, discovered by PC Porter, were laying claim to their own.

'That disposes of all the articles except the gold watch and the pocketbook,' said the sergeant after the claimants had gone, 'gold watch, Elgin half-hunter No 5029020, pocketbook containing no papers, no card, no address, and only three pages of writing. What this means I don't know.' The sergeant handed the book to Howard. The page that puzzled the policeman contained simply a list of streets. Against each street was scrawled a cabalistic character.

'Looks like the diary of a paperchase,' said Mr Howard. 'What is on the other pages?'

They turned the leaf. This was filled with figures.

'H'm,' said the disappointed sergeant, and again turned overleaf. The contents of this page was understandable and readable although evidently written in a hurry as though it had been taken down at dictation.

'The chap who wrote this must have had a train to catch,' said the facetious Mr Howard, pointing to the abbreviations:

> *Will not leave D.S., except for Hs. Will drive to Hs in M.C. (4 dummy brghms first), 8.30. At 2 600 p arve traf divtd Embank, 80 spls. inside D.S. One each rm, three each cor, six basmt, six rf. All drs wide opn allow each off see another, all spls will carry revr. Nobody except F and H to approach R. In Hse strange gal filled with spl, all press vouched for. 200 spl. in cor. If nec battalion guards at disposal.*

The policeman read this over slowly.

'Now what the devil does that mean?' asked the sergeant helplessly.

It was at that precise moment that Constable Howard earned his promotion.

'Let me have that book for ten minutes,' he said excitedly. The sergeant handed the book over with wondering stare.

'I think I can find an owner for this,' said Howard, his hand trembling as he took the book, and ramming his hat on his head he ran out into the street.

He did not stop running until he reached the main road, and finding a cab he sprang in with a hurried order to the driver.

'Whitehall, and drive like blazes,' he called, and in a few minutes he was explaining his errand to the inspector in charge of the cordon that guarded the entrance of Downing Street.

'Constable Howard, 946 L. reserve,' he introduced himself. 'I've a very important message for Superintendent Falmouth.'

That officer, looking tired and beaten, listened to the policeman's story.

'It looks to me,' went on Howard breathlessly, 'as though this has something to do with your case, sir. D.S. is Downing Street, and—' He produced the book and Falmouth snatched at it.

He read a few words and then gave a triumphant cry.

'Our secret instructions,' he cried, and catching the constable by the arm he drew him to the entrance hall.

'Is my car outside? he asked, and in response to a whistle a car drew up. 'Jump in, Howard,' said the detective, and the car slipped into Whitehall.

'Who is the thief?' asked the senior.

'Billy Marks, sir,' replied Howard; 'you may not know him, but down at Lambeth he is a well-known character.'

'Oh, yes,' Falmouth hastened to correct, 'I know Billy very well indeed—we'll see what he has to say.'

The car drew up at the police station and the two men jumped out.

The sergeant rose to his feet as he recognised the famous Falmouth, and saluted.

'I want to see the prisoner Marks,' said Falmouth shortly, and Billy, roused from his sleep, came blinking into the charge office.

'Now, Billy,' said the detective, 'I've got a few words to say to you.'

'Why, it's Mr Falmouth,' said the astonished Billy, and something like fear shaded his face. 'I wasn't in that 'Oxton affair, s'help me.'

'Make your mind easy, Billy; I don't want you for anything, and if you'll answer my questions truthfully, you may get off the present charge and get a reward into the bargain.'

Billy was suspicious.

'I'm not going to give anybody away if that's what you mean,' he said sullenly.

'Nor that either,' said the detective impatiently. 'I want to know where you found this pocketbook,' and he held it up.

Billy grinned.

'Found it lyin' on the pavement,' he lied.

'I want the truth,' thundered Falmouth.

'Well,' said Billy sulkily, 'I pinched it.'

'From whom?'

'I didn't stop to ask him his name,' was the impudent reply.

The detective breathed deeply.

'Now, look here,' he said, lowering his voice, 'you've heard about the Four Just Men?'

Billy nodded, opening his eyes in amazement at the question.

'Well,' exclaimed Falmouth impressively, 'the man to whom this pocketbook belongs is one of them.'

'What!' cried Billy.

'For his capture there is a reward of a thousand pounds offered. If your description leads to his arrest that thousand is yours.'

Marks stood paralysed at the thought.

'A thousand—a thousand?' he muttered in a dazed fashion, 'and I might just as easily have caught him.'

'Come, come!' cried the detective sharply, 'you may catch him yet—tell us what he looked like.'

Billy knitted his brows in thought.

'He looked like a gentleman,' he said, trying to recall from the chaos of his mind a picture of his victim; 'he had a white weskit, a white shirt, nice patent shoes——'

'But his face—his face!' demanded the detective.

'His face?' cried Billy indignantly, 'how do I know what it

97

looked like? I don't look a chap in the face when I'm pinching his watch, do I?'

9

The Cupidity of Marks

'You cursed dolt, you infernal fool!' stormed the detective, catching Billy by the collar and shaking him like a rat. 'Do you mean to tell me that you had one of the Four Just Men in your hand, and did not even take the trouble to look at him?'

Billy wrenched himself free.

'You leave me alone!' he said defiantly. 'How was I to know it was one of the Four Just Men, and how do you know it was?' he added with a cunning twist of his face. Billy's mind was beginning to work rapidly. He saw in this staggering statement of the detective a chance of making capital out of the position which to within a few minutes he had regarded as singularly unfortunate.

'I did get a bit of a glance at 'em,' he said, 'they——'

'Them—they?' said the detective quickly. 'How many were there?'

'Never mind,' said Billy sulkily. He felt the strength of his position.

'Billy,' said the detective earnestly, 'I mean business; if you know anything you've got to tell us.'

'Ho!' cried the prisoner in defiance. 'Got to, 'ave I? Well, I know the lor as well as you—you can't make a chap speak if he don't want. You can't——'

The detective signalled the other police officers to retire, and when they were out of earshot he dropped his voice and said:

'Harry Moss came out last week.'

Billy flushed and lowered his eyes.

'I don't know no Harry Moss,' he muttered doggedly.

'Harry Moss came out last week,' continued the detective shortly, 'after doing three years for robbery with violence—three years and ten lashes.'

'I don't know anything about it,' said Marks in the same tone.

'He got clean away and the police had no clues,' the detective went on remorselessly, 'and they might not have caught him to this day, only—only "from information received" they took him one night out of his bed in Leman Street.'

Billy licked his dry lips, but did not speak.

'Harry Moss would like to know who he owes his three stretch to—and the ten. Men who've had the cat have a long memory, Billy.'

'That's not playing the game, Mr Falmouth,' cried Billy thickly. 'I—I was a bit hard up, an' Harry Moss wasn't a pal of mine—and the p'lice wanted to find out——'

'And the police want to find out now,' said Falmouth.

Billy Marks made no reply for a moment.

'I'll tell you all there is to be told,' he said at last, and cleared his throat. The detective stopped him.

'Not here,' he said. Then turning to the officer in charge:

'Sergeant, you may release this man on bail—I will stand sponsor.' The humorous side of this appealed to Billy at least, for he grinned sheepishly and recovered his former spirits.

'First time I've been baled out by the p'lice,' he remarked facetiously.

The motor-car bore the detective and his charge to Scotland Yard, and in Superintendent Falmouth's office Billy prepared to unburden himself.

'Before you begin,' said the officer, 'I want to warn you that you must be as brief as possible. Every minute is precious.'

So Billy told his story. In spite of the warning there were embellishments, to which the detective was forced to listen impatiently.

At last the pickpocket reached the point.

'There was two of 'em, one a tall chap and one not so tall. I heard one say 'My dear George'—the little one said that, the one I took the ticker from and the pocketbook. Was there anything in the notebook?' Billy asked suddenly.

'Go on,' said the detective.

'Well,' resumed Billy, 'I follered 'em up to the end of the street, and they was waitin' to cross towards Charing Cross Road when I lifted the clock, you understand?'

'What time was this?'

' 'Arf past ten—or it might've been eleven.'

'And you did not see their faces?'

The thief shook his head emphatically.

'If I never get up from where I'm sittin' I didn't, Mr Falmouth,' he said earnestly.

The detective rose with a sigh.

'I'm afraid you're not much use to me, Billy,' he said ruefully. 'Did you notice whether they wore beards, or were they clean-shaven, or——'

Billy shook his head mournfully.

'I could easily tell you a lie, Mr Falmouth,' he said frankly, 'and I could easily pitch a tale that would take you in, but I'm playin' it square with you.'

The detective recognised the sincerity of the man and nodded.

'You've done your best, Billy,' he said, and then: 'I'll tell you what I'm going to do. You are the only man in the world who has ever seen one of the Four Just Men—and lived to tell the story. Now, although you cannot remember his face, perhaps if you met him again in the street you would know him—there may be some little trick of walking, some habit of holding the hands that you cannot recall now, but if you saw again you would recognise. I shall therefore take upon myself the responsibility of releasing you from custody until the day after tomorrow. I want you to find this man you robbed.

101

Here is a sovereign; go home, get a little sleep, turn out as early as you can and go west.' The detective went to his desk, and wrote a dozen words on a card. 'Take this: if you see the man or his companion, follow them, show this card to the first policeman you meet, point out the man, and you'll go to bed a thousand pounds richer than when you woke.'

Billy took the card.

'If you want me at any time you will find somebody here who will know where I am. Goodnight,' and Billy passed into the street, his brain in a whirl, and a warrant written on a visiting card in his waistcoat pocket.

The morning that was to witness great events broke bright and clear over London. Manfred, who, contrary to his usual custom, had spent the night at the workshop in Carnaby Street, watched the dawn from the flat roof of the building.

He lay face downwards, a rug spread beneath him, his head resting on his hands. Dawn with its white, pitiless light, showed his strong face, seamed and haggard. The white streaks in his trim beard were accentuated in the light of morning. He looked tired and disheartened, so unlike his usual self that Gonsalez, who crept up through the trap just before the sun rose, was as near alarmed as it was possible for that phlegmatic man to be. He touched him on the arm and Manfred started.

'What is the matter?' asked Leon softly.

Manfred's smile and shake of head did not reassure the questioner.

'Is it Poiccart and the thief?'

'Yes,' nodded Manfred. Then speaking aloud, he asked: 'Have you ever felt over any of our cases as you feel in this?'

They spoke in such low tones as almost to approach whispering. Gonsalez stared ahead thoughtfully.

'Yes,' he admitted, 'once—the woman at Warsaw. You remember how easy it all seemed, and how circumstance after circumstance thwarted us . . . till I began to feel, as I feel now, that we should fail.'

'No, no, no!' said Manfred fiercely. 'There must be no talk of failure, Leon, no thought of it.'

He crawled to the trapdoor and lowered himself into the corridor, and Gonsalez followed.

'Thery?' he asked.

'Asleep.'

They were entering the studio, and Manfred had his hand on the door handle when a footstep sounded on the bottom floor.

'Who's there?' cried Manfred, and a soft whistle from below sent him flying downstairs.

'Poiccart!' he cried.

Poiccart it was, unshaven, dusty, weary.

'Well?' Manfred's ejaculation was almost brutal in its bluntness.

'Let us go upstairs,' said Poiccart shortly. The three men ascended the dusty stairway, not a word being spoken until they reached the small living-room.

Then Poiccart spoke:

'The very stars in their courses are fighting against us,' he said, throwing himself into the only comfortable chair in the room, and flinging his hat into a corner. 'The man who stole my pocketbook has been arrested by the police. He is a well-known criminal of a sneak-thief order, and unfortunately he had been under observation during the evening. The pocketbook was found in his possession, and all might have been well, but an unusually smart police officer associated the contents with us.

'After I had left you I went home and changed, then made my way to Downing Street. I was one of the curious crowd that stood watching the guarded entrance. I knew that Falmouth was there, and I knew, too, if there was any discovery made it would be communicated immediately to Downing

Street. Somehow I felt sure the man was an ordinary thief, and that if we had anything to fear it was from a chance arrest. Whilst I was waiting a cab dashed up, and out an excited man jumped. He was obviously a policeman, and I had just time to engage a hansom when Falmouth and the new arrival came flying out. I followed them in the cab as fast as possible without exciting the suspicion of the driver. Of course, they out-distanced us, but their destination was evident. I dismissed the cab at the corner of the street in which the police station is situated, and walked down and found, as I had expected, the car drawn up at the door.

'I managed to get a fleeting glance at the charge room—I was afraid that any interrogation there might be would have been conducted in the cell, but by the greatest of good luck they had chosen the charge room. I saw Falmouth, and the policeman, and the prisoner. The latter, a mean-faced, long-jawed man with shifty eyes—no, no, Leon, don't question me about the physiognomy of the man—my view was for photographic purposes—I wanted to remember him.

'In that second I could see the detective's anger, the thief's defiance, and I knew that the man was saying that he could not recognise us.'

'Ha!' It was Manfred's sigh of relief that put a period to Poiccart's speech.

'But I wanted to make sure,' resumed the latter. 'I walked back the way I had come. Suddenly I heard the hum of the car behind me, and it passed me with another passenger. I guessed that they were taking the man back to Scotland Yard.

'I was content to walk back; I was curious to know what the police intended doing with their new recruit. Taking up a station that gave me a view of the entrance of the street, I waited. After a while the man came out alone. His step was light and buoyant. A glimpse I got of his face showed me a strange blending of bewilderment and gratification. He turned on to the Embankment, and I followed close behind.'

'There was a danger that he was being shadowed by the police, too,' said Gonsalez.

'Of that I was well satisfied,' Poiccart rejoined. 'I took a very careful survey before I acted. Apparently the police were content to let him roam free. When he was abreast of the Temple steps he stopped and looked undecidedly left and right, as though he were not quite certain as to what he should do next. At that moment I came abreast of him, passed him, and then turned back, fumbling in my pockets.

' "Can you oblige me with a match?" I asked.

'He was most affable; produced a box of matches and invited me to help myself.

'I took a match, struck it, and lit my cigar, holding the match so that he could see my face.'

'That was wise,' said Manfred gravely.

'It showed his face too, and out of the corner of my eye I watched him searching every feature. But there was no sign of recognition and I began a conversation. We lingered where we had met for a while and then by mutual consent we walked in the direction of Blackfriars, crossed the bridge, chatting on inconsequent subjects, the poor, the weather, the newspapers. On the other side of the bridge is a coffee-stall. I determined to make my next move. I invited him to take a cup of coffee, and when the cups were placed before us, I put down a sovereign. The stall-keeper shook his head, said he could not change it. 'Hasn't your friend any small change?' he asked.

'It was here that the vanity of the little thief told me what I wanted to know. He drew from his pocket, with a nonchalant air—a sovereign. 'This is all that I have got,' he drawled. I found some coppers—I had to think quickly. He had told the police something, something worth paying for—what was it? It could not have been a description of ourselves, for if he had recognised us then, he would have known me when I struck

105

the match and when I stood there, as I did, in the full glare of the light of the coffee-stall. And then a cold fear came to me. Perhaps he had recognised me, and with a thief's cunning was holding me in conversation until he could get assistance to take me.'

Poiccart paused for a moment, and drew a small phial from his pocket; this he placed carefully on the table.

'He was as near to death then as ever he has been in his life,' he said quietly, 'but somehow the suspicion wore away. In our walk we had passed three policemen—there was an opportunity if he had wanted it.

'He drank his coffee and said, "I must be going home."

' "Indeed!" I said. "I suppose I really ought to go home too—I have a lot of work to do tomorrow.' He leered at me. "So have I," he said with a grin, "but whether I can do it or not I don't know."

'We had left the coffee-stall, and now stopped beneath a lamp that stood at the corner of the street.

'I knew that I had only a few seconds to secure the information I wanted—so I played bold and led directly to the subject. "What of these Four Just Men?" I asked, just as he was about to slouch away. He turned back instantly. "What about them?" he asked quickly. I led him on from that by gentle stages to the identity of the Four. He was eager to talk about them, anxious to know what I thought, but most concerned of all about the reward. He was engrossed in the subject, and then suddenly he leant forward, and, tapping me on the chest with a grimy forefinger, he commenced to state a hypothetical case.'

Poiccart stopped to laugh—his laugh ended in a sleepy yawn.

'You know the sort of questions,' said he, 'and you know how very naïve the illiterate are when they are seeking to disguise their identities by elaborate hypotheses. Well, that is the story. He—Marks is his name—thinks he may be able to

106

recognise one of us by some extraordinary trick of memory. To enable him to do this, he has been granted freedom— tomorrow he would search London, he said.'

'A full day's work,' laughed Manfred.

'Indeed,' agreed Poiccart soberly, 'but hear the sequel. We parted, and I walked westward perfectly satisfied of our security. I made for Covent Garden Market, because this is one of the places in London where a man may be seen at four o'clock in the morning without exciting suspicion.

'I had strolled through the market, idly watching the busy scene, when, for some cause that I cannot explain, I turned suddenly on my heel and came face to face with Marks! He grinned sheepishly, and recognised me with a nod of his head.

'He did not wait for me to ask him his business, but started in to explain his presence.

'I accepted his explanation easily, and for the second time that night invited him to coffee. He hesitated at first, then accepted. When the coffee was brought, he pulled it to him as far from my reach as possible, and then I knew that Mr Marks had placed me at fault, that I had underrated his intelligence, that all the time he had been unburdening himself he had recognised me. He had put me off my guard.'

'But why——?' began Manfred.

'That is what I thought,' the other answered. 'Why did he not have me arrested?' He turned to Leon, who had been a silent listener. 'Tell us, Leon, why?'

'The explanation is simple,' said Gonsalez quietly: 'why did not Thery betray us?—cupidity, the second most potent force of civilisation. He has some doubt of the reward. He may fear the honesty of the police—most criminals do so; he may want witnesses.' Leon walked to the wall, where his coat hung. He buttoned it thoughtfully, ran his hand over his smooth chin, then pocketed the little phial that stood on the table.

'You have slipped him, I suppose?' he asked.

Poiccard nodded.

'He lives——?'

'At 700 Red Cross Street, in the Borough—it is a common lodging-house.'

Leon took a pencil from the table and rapidly sketched a head upon the edge of a newspaper.

'Like this?' he asked.

Poiccart examined the portrait.

'Yes,' he said in surprise; 'have you seen him?'

'No,' said Leon carelessly, 'but such a man would have such a head.'

He paused on the threshold.

'I think it is necessary.' There was a question in his assertion. It was addressed rather to Manfred, who stood with his folded arms and knit brow staring at the floor.

For answer Manfred extended his clenched fist.

Leon saw the down-turned thumb, and left the room.

*   *   *

Billy Marks was in a quandary. By the most innocent device in the world his prey had managed to slip through his fingers. When Poiccart, stopping at the polished doors of the best hotel in London, whither they had strolled, casually remarked that he would not be a moment and disappeared into the hotel, Billy was nonplussed. This was a contingency for which he was not prepared. He had followed the suspect from Blackfriars; he was almost sure that this was the man he had robbed. He might, had he wished, have called upon the first constable he met to take the man into custody; but the suspicion of the thief, the fear that he might be asked to share the reward with the man who assisted him restrained him. And besides, it might not be the man at all, argued Billy, and yet——

Poiccart was a chemist, a man who found joy in unhealthy

108

precipitates, who mixed evil-smelling drugs and distilled, filtered, carbonated, oxydised, and did all manner of things in glass tubes, to the vegetable, animal, and mineral products of the earth.

Billy had left Scotland Yard to look for a man with a discoloured hand. Here again, he might, had he been less fearful of treachery, have placed in the hands of the police a very valuable mark of identification.

It seems a very lame excuse to urge on Billy's behalf that this cupidity alone stayed his hand when he came face to face with the man he was searching for. And yet it was so. Then again there was a sum in simple proportion to be worked out. If one Just Man was worth a thousand pounds, what was the commercial value of four? Billy was a thief with a business head. There were no waste products in his day's labour. He was not a conservative scoundrel who stuck to one branch of his profession. He would pinch a watch, or snatch a till, or pass snide florins with equal readiness. He was a butterfly of crime, flitting from one illicit flower to another, and not above figuring as the X of 'information received'.

So that when Poiccard disappeared within the magnificent portals of the Royal Hotel in Northumberland Avenue, Billy was hipped. He realised in a flash that his captive had gone whither he could not follow without exposing his hand; that the chances were he had gone for ever. He looked up and down the street; there was no policeman in sight. In the vestibule, a porter in shirt sleeves was polishing brasses. It was still very early; the streets were deserted, and Billy, after a few moment's hesitation, took a course that he would not have dared at a more conventional hour.

He pushed open the swing doors and passed into the vestibule. The porter turned on him as he entered and favoured him with a suspicious frown.

'What do you want?' asked he, eyeing the tattered coat of the visitor in some disfavour.

'Look 'ere, old feller,' began Billy, in his most conciliatory tone.

Just then the porter's strong right arm caught him by the coat collar, and Billy found himself stumbling into the street.

'Outside—you,' said the porter firmly.

It needed this rebuff to engender in Marks the necessary self-assurance to carry him through.

Straightening his ruffled clothing, he pulled Falmouth's card from his pocket and returned to the charge with dignity.

'I am a p'lice officer,' he said, adopting the opening that he knew so well, 'and if you interfere with me, look out, young feller!'

The porter took the card and scrutinised it.

'What do you want?' he asked in more civil tones. He would have added 'sir', but somehow it stuck in his throat. If the man is a detective, he argued to himself, he is very well disguised.

'I want that gentleman that came in before me,' said Billy.

The porter scratched his head.

'What is the number of his room?' he asked.

'Never mind about the number of his room,' said Billy rapidly. 'Is there any back way to this hotel—any way a man can get out of it? I mean, besides through the front entrance?'

'Half a dozen,' replied the porter.

Billy groaned.

'Take me round to one of them, will you?' he asked. And the porter led the way.

One of the tradesmen's entrances was from a small back street; and here it was that a street scavenger gave the information that Marks had feared. Five minutes before a man answering to the description had walked out, turned towards the Strand and, picking up a cab in the sight of the street cleaner, had driven off.

Baffled, and with the added bitterness that had he played boldly he might have secured at any rate a share of a thousand pounds, Billy walked slowly to the Embankment, cursing the folly that had induced him to throw away the fortune that was in his hands. With hands thrust deep into his pockets, he tramped the weary length of the Embankment, going over again and again the incidents of the night and each time muttering a lurid condemnation of his error. It must have been an hour after he had lost Poiccart that it occurred to him all was not lost. He had the man's description, he had looked at his face, he knew him feature by feature. That was something, at any rate. Nay, it occurred to him that if the man was arrested through his description he would still be entitled to the reward—or a part of it. He dared not see Falmouth and tell him that he had been in company with the man all night without effecting his arrest. Falmouth would never believe him, and, indeed, it was curious that he should have met him.

This fact struck Billy for the first time. By what strange chance had he met this man? Was it possible—the idea frightened Marks—that the man he had robbed had recognised him, and that he had deliberately sought him out with murderous intent?

A cold perspiration broke upon the narrow forehead of the thief. These men were murderers, cruel, relentless murderers: suppose——?

He turned from the contemplation of the unpleasant possibilities to meet a man who was crossing the road towards him. He eyed the stranger doubtingly. The newcomer was a young-looking man, clean-shaven, with sharp features and restless blue eyes. As he came closer, Marks noted that first appearance had been deceptive; the man was not so young as he looked. He might have been forty, thought Marks. He approached, looked hard at Billy, then beckoned him to stop, for Billy was walking away.

'Is your name Marks?' asked the stranger authoritatively.

'Yes, sir,' replied the thief.

111

'Have you seen Mr Falmouth?'

'Not since last night,' replied Marks in surprise.

'Then you are to come at once to him.'

'Where is he?'

'At Kensington Police Station—there has been an arrest, and he wants you to identify the man.'

Billy's heart sank.

'Do I get any of the reward?' he demanded, 'that is if I recognise 'im?'

The other nodded and Billy's hopes rose.

'You must follow me,' said the newcomer, 'Mr Falmouth does not wish us to be seen together. Take a first-class ticket to Kensington and get into the next carriage to mine—come.'

He turned and crossed the road toward Charing Cross, and Billy followed at a distance.

He found the stranger pacing the platform and gave no sign of recognition. A train pulled into the station and Marks followed his conductor through a crowd of workmen the train had discharged. He entered an empty first-class carriage, and Marks, obeying instructions, took possession of the adjoining compartment, and found himself the solitary occupant.

Between Charing Cross and Westminster Marks had time to review his position. Between the last station and St James's Park, he invented his excuses to the detective; between the Park and Victoria he had completed his justification for a share of the reward. Then as the train moved into the tunnel for its five minutes' run to Sloane Square, Billy noticed a draught, and turned his head to see the stranger standing on the footboard of the swaying carriage, holding the half-opened door.

Marks was startled.

'Pull up the window on your side,' ordered the man, and Billy, hypnotised by the authoritative voice, obeyed. At that moment he heard the tinkle of broken glass.

He turned with an angry snarl.

'What's the game?' he demanded.

For answer the stranger swung himself clear of the door and, closing it softly, disappeared.

'What's his game?' repeated Marks drowsily. Looking down he saw a broken phial at his feet, by the phial lay a shining sovereign. He stared stupidly at it for a moment, then, just before the train ran into Victoria Station, he stooped to pick it up. . . .

10

Three Who Died

A passenger leisurely selecting his compartment during the wait at Kensington opened a carriage door and staggered back coughing. A solicitous porter and an alarmed station official ran forward and pulled open the door, and the sickly odour of almonds pervaded the station.

A little knot of passengers gathered and peered over one another's shoulders, whilst the station inspector investigated. By and by came a doctor, and a stretcher, and a policeman from the street without.

Together they lifted the huddled form of a dead man from the carriage and laid it on the platform.

'Did you find anything?' asked the policeman.

'A sovereign and a broken bottle,' was the reply.

The policeman fumbled in the dead man's pockets.

'I don't suppose he'll have any papers to show who he is,' he said with knowledge. 'Here's a first-class ticket—it must be a case of suicide. Here's a card——'

He turned it over and read it, and his face underwent a change.

He gave a few hurried instructions, then made his way to the nearest telegraph office.

Superintendent Falmouth, who had snatched a few hours' sleep at the Downing Street house, rose with a troubled mind and an uneasy feeling that in spite of all his precautions the day would end disastrously. He was hardly dressed before the arrival of the Assistant Commissioner was announced.

'I have your report, Falmouth,' was the official's greeting;

'you did perfectly right to release Marks—have you had news of him this morning?'

'No.'

'H'm,' said the Commissioner thoughtfully. 'I wonder whether——' He did not finish his sentence. 'Has it occurred to you that the Four may have realised their danger?'

The detective's face showed surprise.

'Why, of course, sir.'

'Have you considered what their probable line of action will be?'

'N—no—unless it takes the form of an attempt to get out of the country.'

'Has it struck you that whilst this man Marks is looking for them, they are probably seeking him?'

'Billy is smart,' said the detective uneasily.

'So are they,' said the Commissioner with an emphatic nod. 'My advice is, get in touch with Marks and put two of your best men to watch him.'

'That shall be done at once,' replied Falmouth; 'I am afraid that it is a precaution that should have been taken before.'

'I am going to see Sir Philip,' the Commissioner went on, and he added with a dubious smile, 'I shall be obliged to frighten him a little.'

'What is the idea?'

'We wish him to drop this Bill. Have you seen the morning papers?'

'No, sir.'

'They are unanimous that the Bill should be abandoned—they say because it is not sufficiently important to warrant the risk, that the country itself is divided on its merit; but as a matter of fact they are afraid of the consequence; and upon my soul I'm a little afraid too.'

He mounted the stairs, and was challenged at the landing by one of his subordinates.

This was a system introduced after the episode of the

disguised 'detective'. The Foreign Minister was now in a state of siege. Nobody had to be trusted, a password had been initiated, and every precaution taken to ensure against a repetition of the previous mistake.

His hand was raised to knock upon the panel of the study, when he felt his arm gripped. He turned to see Falmouth with white face and startled eyes.

'They've finished Billy,' said the detective breathlessly. 'He has just been found in a railway carriage at Kensington.'

The Commissioner whistled.

'How was it done?' he asked.

Falmouth was the picture of haggard despair.

'Prussic acid gas,' he said bitterly; 'they are scientific. Look you, sir, persuade this man to drop his damned Bill.'

He pointed to the door of Sir Philip's room. 'We shall never save him. I have got the feeling in my bones that he is a doomed man.'

'Nonsense!' the Commissioner answered sharply. 'You are growing nervous—you haven't had enough sleep, Falmouth. That isn't spoken like your real self—we *must* save him.'

He turned from the study and beckoned one of the officers who guarded the landing.

'Sergeant, tell Inspector Collins to send an emergency call throughout the area for reserves to gather immediately. I will put such a cordon round Ramon today,' he went on addressing Falmouth, 'that no man shall reach him without the fear of being crushed to death.'

And within an hour there was witnessed in London a scene that has no parallel in the history of the Metropolis. From every district there came a small army of policemen. They arrived by train, by tramway car, by motorbus, by every vehicle and method of traction that could be requisitioned or seized. They streamed from the stations, they poured through the thoroughfares, till London stood aghast at the realisation of the strength of her civic defences.

116

Whitehall was soon packed from end to end; St James's Park was black with them. Automatically Whitehall, Charles Street, Birdcage Walk, and the eastern end of the Mall were barred to all traffic by solid phalanxes of mounted constables. St George's Street was in the hands of the force, the roof of every house was occupied by a uniformed man. Not a house or room that overlooked in the slightest degree the Foreign Secretary's residence but was subjected to a rigorous search. It was as though martial law had been proclaimed, and indeed two regiments of Guards were under arms the whole of the day ready for any emergency. In Sir Philip's room the Commissioner, backed by Falmouth, made his last appeal to the stubborn man whose life was threatened.

'I tell you, sir,' said the Commissioner earnestly, 'we can do no more than we have done, and I am still afraid. These men affect me as would something supernatural. I have a horrible dread that for all our precautions we have left something out of our reckoning; that we are leaving unguarded some avenue which by their devilish ingenuity they may utilise. The death of this man Marks has unnerved me—the Four are ubiquitous as well as omnipotent. I beg of you, sir, for God's sake, think well before you finally reject their terms. Is the passage of this Bill so absolutely necessary?'—he paused—'is it worth your life?' he asked with blunt directness; and the crudity of the question made Sir Philip wince.

He waited some time before he replied, and when he spoke his voice was low and firm.

'I shall not withdraw,' he said slowly, with a dull, dogged evenness of tone. 'I shall not withdraw in any circumstance.

'I have gone too far,' he went on, raising his hand to check Falmouth's appeal. 'I have got beyond fear, I have even got beyond resentment; it is now to me a question of justice. Am I right in introducing a law that will remove from this country colonies of dangerously intelligent criminals, who, whilst enjoying immunity from arrest, urge ignorant men forward

117

to commit acts of violence and treason? If I am right, the Four Just Men are wrong. Or are they right: is this measure an unjust thing, an act of tyranny, a piece of barbarism dropped into the very centre of twentieth-century thought, an anachronism? If these men are right, then I am wrong. So it has come to this, that I have to satisfy my mind as to the standard of right and wrong that I must accept—and I accept my own.'

He met the wondering gaze of the officers with a calm, unflinching countenance.

'You were wise to take the precautions you have,' he resumed quietly. 'I have been foolish to chafe under your protective care.'

'We must take even further precautions,' the Commissioner interrupted; 'between six and half past eight o'clock tonight we wish you to remain in your study, and under no circumstance to open the door to a single person—even to myself or Mr Falmouth. During that time you must keep your door locked.' He hesitated. 'If you would rather have one of us with you——'

'No, no,' was the Minister's quick reply; 'after the impersonation of yesterday I would rather be alone.'

The Commissioner nodded. 'This room is anarchist-proof,' he said, waving his hand round the apartment. 'During the night we have made a thorough inspection, examined the floors, the wall, the ceiling, and fixed steel shields to the shutters.'

He looked round the chamber with the scrutiny of a man to whom every visible object was familiar.

Then he noticed something new had been introduced. On the table stood a blue china bowl full of roses.

'This is new,' he said, bending his head to catch the fragrance of the beautiful flowers.

'Yes,' was Ramon's careless reply, 'they were sent from my house in Hereford this morning.'

118

The Commissioner plucked a leaf from one of the blooms and rolled it between his fingers. 'They look so real,' he said paradoxically, 'that they might even be artificial.'

As he spoke he was conscious that he associated the roses in some way with—what?

He passed slowly down the noble marble stairway—a policeman stood on every other step—and gave his views to Falmouth.

'You cannot blame the old man for his decision; in fact, I admire him today more than I have ever done before. But'— there was a sudden solemnity in his voice—'I am afraid—I am afraid.'

Falmouth said nothing.

'The notebook tells nothing,' the Commissioner continued, 'save the route that Sir Philip might have taken had he been anxious to arrive at 44 Downing Street by back streets. The futility of the plan is almost alarming, for there is so much evidence of a strong subtle mind behind the seeming innocence of this list of streets that I am confident that we have not got hold of the true inwardness of its meaning.'

He passed into the streets and threaded his way between crowds of policemen. The extraordinary character of the precautions taken by the police had the natural result of keeping the general public ignorant of all that was happening in Downing Street. Reporters were prohibited within the magic circle, and newspapers, and particularly the evening newspapers, had to depend upon such information as was grudgingly offered by Scotland Yard. This was scanty, while their clues and theories, which were many, were various and wonderful.

The *Megaphone*, the newspaper that regarded itself as being the most directly interested in the doings of the Four Just Men, strained every nerve to obtain news of the latest developments. With the coming of the fatal day, excitement had reached an extraordinary pitch; every fresh edition of the

119

evening newspapers was absorbed as soon as it reached the streets. There was little material to satisfy the appetite of a sensation-loving public, but such as there was, was given. Pictures of 44 Downing Street, portraits of the Minister, plans of the vicinity of the Foreign Office, with diagrams illustrating existing police precautions, stood out from columns of letterpress dealing, not for the first but for the dozenth time, with the careers of the Four as revealed by their crimes.

And with curiosity at its height, and all London, all England, the whole of the civilised world, talking of one thing and one thing only there came like a bombshell the news of Marks' death.

Variously described as one of the detectives engaged in the case, as a foreign police officer, as Falmouth himself, the death of Marks grew from 'Suicide in a Railway Carriage' to its real importance. Within an hour the story of tragedy, inaccurate in detail, true in substance, filled the columns of the Press. Mystery on mystery! Who was this ill-dressed man, what part was he playing in the great game, how came he by his death? asked the world instantly; and little by little, pieced together by ubiquitous newsmen, the story was made known. On top of this news came the great police march on Whitehall. Here was evidence of the serious view the authorities were taking.

'From my vantage place,' wrote Smith in the *Megaphone*, 'I could see the length of Whitehall. It was the most wonderful spectacle that London has ever witnessed. I saw nothing but a great sea of black helmets reaching from one end of the broad thoroughfare to the other. Police! the whole vicinity was black with police; they thronged side streets, they crowded into the Park, they formed not a cordon, but a mass through which it was impossible to penetrate.'

For the Commissioners of Police were leaving nothing to chance. If they were satisfied that cunning could be matched by cunning, craft by craft, stealth by counterstealth, they would have been content to defend their charge on conventional lines. But they were outmanœuvred. The stake was too high to depend upon strategy—this was a case that demanded brute force. It is difficult, writing so long after the event, to realise how the terror of the Four had so firmly fastened upon the finest police organisation in the world, to appreciate the panic that had come upon a body renowned for its clear-headedness.

The crowd that blocked the approaches to Whitehall soon began to grow as the news of Billy's death circulated, and soon after two o'clock that afternoon, by order of the Commissioner, Westminster Bridge was closed to all traffic, vehicular or passenger. The section of the Embankment that runs between Westminster and Hungerford Bridge was next swept by the police and cleared of curious pedestrians; Northumberland Avenue was barred, and before three o'clock there was no space within five hundred yards of the official residence of Sir Philip Ramon that was not held by a representative of the law. Members of Parliament on their way to the House were escorted by mounted men, and, taking on a reflected glory, were cheered by the crowd. All that afternoon a hundred thousand people waited patiently, seeing nothing, save, towering above the heads of a host of constabulary, the spires and towers of the Mother of Parliaments, or the blank faces of the buildings—in Trafalgar Square, along the Mall as far as the police would allow them, at the lower end of Victoria Street, eight deep along the Albert Embankment, growing in volume every hour. London waited, waited in patience, orderly, content to stare stead-fastly at nothing, deriving no satisfaction for their weariness but the sense of being as near as it was humanly possible to be to the scene of a tragedy. A stranger arriving in London, bewildered by this gathering, asked for the cause. A man standing on the outskirts of the Embankment throng pointed

121

across the river with the stem of his pipe.

'We're waiting for a man to be murdered,' he said simply, as one who describes a familiar function.

About the edge of these throngs newspaper boys drove a steady trade. From hand to hand the pink sheets were passed over the heads of the crowd. Every half hour brought a new edition, a new theory, a new description of the scene in which they themselves were playing an ineffectual if picturesque part. The clearing of the Thames Embankment produced an edition; the closing of Westminster Bridge brought another; the arrest of a foolish Socialist who sought to harangue the crowd in Trafalgar Square was worthy of another. Every incident of the day was faithfully recorded and industriously devoured.

All that afternoon they waited, telling and retelling the story of the Four, theorising, speculating, judging. And they spoke of the culmination as one speaks of a promised spectacle, watching the slow-moving hands of Big Ben ticking off the laggard minutes. 'Only two more hours to wait,' they said at six o'clock, and that sentence, or rather the tone of pleasurable anticipation in which it was said, indicated the spirit of the mob. For a mob is a cruel thing, heartless and unpitying.

Seven o'clock boomed forth, and the angry hum of talk ceased. London watched in silence, and with a quicker beating heart, the last hour crawl round the great clock's dial.

There had been a slight alteration in the arrangements at Downing Street, and it was after seven o'clock before Sir Philip, opening the door of his study, in which he had sat alone, beckoned the Commissioner and Falmouth to approach. They walked towards him, stopping a few feet from where he stood.

The Minister was pale, and there were lines on his face that had not been there before. But the hand that held the printed paper was steady and his face was sphinxlike.

122

'I am about to lock my door,' he said calmly. 'I presume that the arrangements we have agreed upon will be carried out?'

'Yes, sir,' answered the Commissioner quietly.

Sir Philip was about to speak, but he checked himself. After a moment he spoke again.

'I have been a just man according to my lights,' he said half to himself. 'Whatever happens I am satisfied that I am doing the right thing—What is that?'

Through the corridor there came a faint roar.

'The people—they are cheering you,' said Falmouth, who just before had made a tour of inspection.

The Minister's lip curled in disdain and the familiar acid crept into his voice.

'They will be terribly disappointed if nothing happens,' he said bitterly. 'The people! God save me from the people, their sympathy, their applause, their insufferable pity.'

He turned and pushed open the door of his study, slowly closed the heavy portal, and the two men heard the snick of the lock as he turned the key.

Falmouth looked at his watch.

'Forty minutes,' was his laconic comment.

*   *   *

In the dark stood the Four Men.

'It is nearly time,' said the voice of Manfred, and Thery shuffled forward and groped on the floor for something.

'Let me strike a match,' he grumbled in Spanish.

'No!'

It was Poiccart's sharp voice that arrested him; it was Gonsalez who stooped quickly and passed sensitive fingers over the floor.

He found one wire and placed it in Thery's hand, then he reached up and found the other, and Thery deftly tied them together.

123

'Is it not time?' asked Thery, short of breath from his exertions.

'Wait.'

Manfred was examining the illuminated dial of his watch. In silence they waited.

'It is time,' said Manfred solemnly, and Thery stretched out his hand.

Stretched out his hand—and groaned and collapsed.

The three heard the groan, felt rather than saw the swaying figure of the man, and heard the thud of him as he struck the floor.

'What has happened?' whispered a tremorless voice; it was Gonsalez.

Manfred was at Thery's side fumbling at his shirt.

'Thery has bungled and paid the consequence,' he said in a hushed voice.

'But Ramon——'

'We shall see, we shall see,' said Manfred, still with his fingers over the heart of the fallen man.

*　　*　　*

That forty minutes was the longest that Falmouth ever remembered spending. He had tried to pass it pleasantly by recounting some of the famous criminal cases in which he had played a leading rôle. But he found his tongue wandering after his mind. He grew incoherent, almost hysterical. The word had been passed round that there was to be no talking in tones above a whisper, and absolute silence reigned, save an occasional sibilant murmur as a necessary question was asked or answered.

Policemen were established in every room, on the roof, in the basement, in every corridor, and each man was armed. Falmouth looked round. He sat in the secretary's office, having arranged for Hamilton to be at the House. Every door

124

stood wide open, wedged back, so that no group of policemen should be out of sight of another.

'I cannot think what can happen,' he whispered for the twentieth time to his superior. 'It is impossible for those fellows to keep their promise—absolutely impossible.'

'The question, to my mind, is whether they will keep their other promise,' was the Commissioner's reply, 'whether having found that they have failed they will give up their attempt. One thing is certain,' he proceeded, 'if Ramon comes out of this alive, his rotten Bill will pass without opposition.'

He looked at his watch. To be exact, he had held his watch in his hand since Sir Philip had entered his room.

'It wants five minutes.' He sighed anxiously.

He walked softly to the door of Sir Philip's room and listened.

'I can hear nothing,' he said.

The next five minutes passed more slowly than any of the preceding.

'It is just on the hour,' said Falmouth in a strained voice. 'We have——'

The distant chime of Big Ben boomed once.

'The hour!' he whispered, and both men listened.

'Two,' muttered Falmouth, counting the strokes.

'Three.'

'Four.'

'Five—what's that?' he muttered quickly.

'I heard nothing—yes, I heard something.' He sprang to the door and bent his head to the level of the keyhole. 'What is that? What——'

Then from the room came a quick, sharp cry of pain, a crash—and silence.

'Quick—this way, men!' shouted Falmouth, and threw his weight against the door.

It did not yield a fraction of an inch.

'Together!'

Three burly constables flung themselves against the panels, and the door smashed open.

Falmouth and the Commissioner ran into the room.

'My God!' cried Falmouth in horror.

Sprawled across the table at which he had been sitting was the figure of the Foreign Secretary.

The paraphernalia that littered his table had been thrown to the floor as in a struggle.

The Commissioner stepped to the fallen man and raised him. One look at the face was sufficient.

'Dead!' he whispered hoarsely. He looked around—save for the police and the dead man the room was empty.

11

A Newspaper Cutting

The court was again crowded today in anticipation of the evidence of the Assistant Commissioner of Police and Sir Francis Katling, the famous surgeon.

Before the proceedings recommenced the Coroner remarked that he had received a great number of letters from all kinds of people containing theories, some of them peculiarly fantastic, as to the cause of Sir Philip Ramon's death.

'The police inform me that they are eager to receive suggestions,' said the Coroner, 'and will welcome any view however bizarre.'

The Assistant Commissioner of Police was the first witness called, and gave in detail the story of the events that had led up to the finding of the late Secretary's dead body. He then went on to describe the appearance of the room. Heavy bookcases filled two sides of the room, the third or south-west was pierced with three windows, the fourth was occupied by a case containing maps arranged on the roller principle.

Were the windows fastened?—Yes.

And adequately protected?—Yes; by wooden folding shutters sheathed with steel.

Was there any indication that these had been tampered with?—None whatever.

Did you institute a search of the room?—Yes; a minute search.

By the Foreman of the Jury: Immediately?—Yes; after the body was removed every article of furniture was taken out of the room, the carpets were taken up, and the walls and ceilings stripped.

And nothing was found?—Nothing.

Is there a fireplace in the room?—Yes.

Was there any possibility of any person effecting an entrance by that method?—Absolutely none.

You have seen the newspapers?—Yes; some of them.

You have seen the suggestion put forward that the deceased was slain by the introduction of a deadly gas?—Yes.

Was that possible?—I hardly think so.

By the Foreman: Did you find any means by which such a gas could be introduced?—(The witness hesitated.) None, except an old disused gaspipe that had an opening above the desk. (Sensation.)

Was there any indication of the presence of such a gas?—Absolutely none.

No smell?—None whatever.

But there are gases which are at once deadly and scentless—carbon dioxide, for example?—Yes; there are.

By the Foreman: Did you test the atmosphere for the presence of such a gas?—No; but I entered the room before it would have had time to dissipate; I should have noticed it.

Was the room disarranged in any way?—Except for the table there was no disarrangement.

Did you find the contents of the table disturbed?—Yes.

Will you describe exactly the appearance of the table?—One or two heavy articles of table furniture, such as the silver candlesticks, etc., alone remained in their positions. On the floor were a number of papers, the inkstand, a pen, and (here the witness drew a notecase from his pocket and extracted a small black shrivelled object) a smashed flower bowl and a number of roses.

Did you find anything in the dead man's hand?—Yes, I found this.

The detective held up a withered rosebud, and a thrill of horror ran through the court.

That is a rose?—Yes.

The Coroner consulted the Commissioner's written report.

Did you notice anything peculiar about the hand?—Yes, where the flower had been there was a round black stain. (Sensation.)

Can you account for that?—No.

By the Foreman: What steps did you take when you discovered this?—I had the flowers carefully collected and as much of the water as was possible absorbed by clean blotting-paper: these were sent to the Home Office for analysis.

Do you know the result of that analysis?—So far as I know, it has revealed nothing.

Did the analysis include leaves from the rose you have in your possession?—Yes.

The Assistant Commissioner then went on to give details of the police arrangements for the day. It was impossible, he emphatically stated, for any person to have entered or left 44 Downing Street without being observed. Immediately after the murder the police on duty were ordered to stand fast. Most of the men, said the witness, were on duty for twenty-six hours at a stretch.

At this stage there was revealed the most sensational feature of the inquiry. It came with dramatic suddenness, and was the result of a question put by the Coroner, who constantly referred to the Commissioner's signed statement that lay before him.

You know of a man called Thery?—Yes.

He was one of a band calling themselves 'The Four Just Men'?—I believe so.

A reward was offered for his apprehension?—Yes.

He was suspected of complicity in the plot to murder Sir Philip Ramon?—Yes.

Has he been found?—Yes.

This monosyllabic reply drew a spontaneous cry of surprise from the crowded court.

When was he found?—This morning.

Where?—On Romney Marshes.

Was he dead?—Yes. (Sensation.)

Was there anything peculiar about the body? (The whole court waited for the answer with bated breath.)—Yes; on his right palm was a stain similar to that found on the hand of Sir Philip Ramon!

A shiver ran through the crowd of listeners.

Was a rose found in his hand also?—No.

By the Foreman: Was there any indication how Thery came to where he was found?—None.

The witness added that no papers or documents of any kind were found upon the man.

Sir Francis Katling was the next witness.

He was sworn and was accorded permission to give his evidence from the solicitor's table, on which he had spread the voluminous notes of his observations. For half an hour he devoted himself to a purely technical record of his examinations. There were three possible causes of death. It might have been natural: the man's weak heart was sufficient to cause such; it might have been by asphyxiation; it might have been the result of a blow that by some extraordinary means left no contusion.

There were no traces of poison?—None.

You have heard the evidence of the last witness?—Yes.

And that portion of the evidence that dealt with a black stain?—Yes.

Did you examine that stain?—Yes.

Have you formed any theories regarding it?—Yes; it seems to me as if it were formed by an acid.

Carbolic acid, for instance?—Yes; but there was no indication of any of the acids of commerce.

You saw the man Thery's hand?—Yes.

Was the stain of a similar character?—Yes, but larger and more irregular.

Were there any signs of acid?—None.

By the Foreman: You have seen many of the fantastic theories put forward by the Press and public?—Yes; I have paid careful attention to them.

And you see nothing in them that would lead you to believe that the deceased met his end by the method suggested?—No.

Gas?—Impossible; it must have been immediately detected.

The introduction into the room of some subtle poison that would asphyxiate and leave no trace?—Such a drug is unknown to medical science.

You have seen the rose found in Sir Philip's hand?—Yes.

How do you account for that?—I cannot account for it.

Nor for the stain?—No.

By the Foreman: You have formed no definite opinion regarding the cause of death?—No; I merely submit one of the three suggestions I have offered.

Are you a believer in hypnotism?—Yes, to a certain extent.

In hypnotic suggestion?—Again, to a certain extent.

Is it possible that the suggestion of death coming at a certain hour so persistently threatened might have led to death?—I do not quite understand you.

Is it possible that the deceased is a victim to hypnotic suggestion?—I do not believe it possible.

By the Foreman: You speak of a blow leaving no contusion. In your experience have you ever seen such a case?—Yes; twice.

But a blow sufficient to cause death?—Yes.

Without leaving a bruise or any mark whatever?—Yes; I saw a case in Japan where a man by exerting a peculiar pressure on the throat produced instant death.

Is that ordinary?—No; it is very unordinary; sufficiently so to create a considerable stir in medical circles. The case was recorded in the *British Medical Journal* in 1896.

And there was no contusion or bruise?—Absolutely none whatever.

The famous surgeon then read a long extract from the *British Medical Journal* bearing out this statement.

Would you say that the deceased died in this way?—It is possible.

By the Foreman: Do you advance that as a serious possibility?—Yes.

With a few more questions of a technical character the examination closed.

As the great surgeon left the box there was a hum of conversation, and keen disappointment was felt on all sides. It had been hoped that the evidence of the medical expert would have thrown light into dark places, but it left the mystery of Sir Philip Ramon's death as far from explanation as ever.

Superintendent Falmouth was the next witness called.

The detective, who gave his evidence in clear tones, was evidently speaking under stress of very great emotion. He seemed to appreciate very keenly the failure of the police to safeguard the life of the dead Minister. It is an open secret that immediately after the tragedy both the officer and the Assistant Commissioner tendered their resignations, which, at the express instruction of the Prime Minister, were not accepted.

Mr Falmouth repeated a great deal of the evidence already given by the Commissioner, and told the story of how he had stood on duty outside the Foreign Secretary's door at the moment of the tragedy. As he detailed the events of that evening a deathly silence came upon the court.

You say you heard a noise proceeding from the study?—Yes.

What sort of a noise?—Well, it is hard to describe what I heard; it was one of those indefinite noises that sounded like a chair being pulled across a soft surface.

Would it be a noise like the sliding of a door or panel?—Yes. (Sensation.)

That is the noise as you described it in your report?—Yes.

Was any panel discovered?—No.

Or any sliding door?—No.

Would it have been possible for a person to have secreted himself in any of the bureaux or bookcases?—No; these were examined.

What happened next?—I heard a click and a cry from Sir Philip, and endeavoured to burst open the door.

By the Foreman: It was locked?—Yes.

And Sir Philip was alone?—Yes; it was by his wish: a wish expressed earlier in the day.

After the tragedy did you make a systematic search both inside and outside the house?—Yes.

Did you make any discovery?—None, except that I made a discovery curious in itself, but having no possible bearing on the case now.

What was this?—Well, it was the presence on the window-sill of the room of two dead sparrows.

Were these examined?—Yes; but the surgeon who disected them gave the opinion that they died from exposure and had fallen from the parapet above.

Was there any trace of poison in these birds?—None that could be discovered.

At this point Sir Francis Katling was recalled. He had seen the birds. He could find no trace of poison.

Granted the possibility of such a gas as we have already spoken of—a deadly gas with the property of rapid dissipation—might not the escape of a minute quantity of such a fume bring about the death of these birds?—Yes, if they were resting on the window-sill.

By the Foreman: Do you connect these birds with the tragedy?—I do not, replied the witness emphatically.

Superintendent Falmouth resumed his evidence.

133

Were there any other curious features that struck you?—None.

The Coroner proceeded to question the witness concerning the relations of Marks with the police.

Was the stain found on Sir Philip's hand, and on the hand of the man Thery, found also on Marks?—No.

*   *   *

It was as the court was dispersing, and little groups of men stood discussing the most extraordinary verdict ever given by a coroner's jury, 'Death from some unknown cause, and wilful murder against some person or persons unknown', that the Coroner himself met on the threshold of the court a familiar face.

'Hullo, Carson!' he said in surprise, 'you here too; I should have thought that your bankrupts kept you busy—even on a day like this—extraordinary case.'

'Extraordinary,' agreed the other.

'Were you there all the time?'

'Yes,' replied the spectator.

'Did you notice what a bright foreman we had?'

'Yes; I think he would make a smarter lawyer than a company promoter.'

'You know him, then?'

'Yes,' yawned the Official Receiver; 'poor devil, he thought he was going to set the Thames on fire, floated a company to reproduce photogravures and things—took Etherington's off our hands, but it's back again.'

'Has he failed?' asked the Coroner in surprise.

'Not exactly failed. He's just given it up, says the climate doesn't suit him—what is his name again?'

'Manfred,' said the Coroner.

12

Conclusion

Falmouth sat on the opposite side of the Chief Commissioner's desk, his hands clasped before him. On the blotting-pad lay a thin sheet of grey notepaper.

The Commissioner picked it up again and re-read it.

> *When you receive this* [it ran] *we who for want of a better title call ourselves The Four Just Men will be scattered throughout Europe, and there is little likelihood of your ever tracing us. In no spirit of boastfulness we say: We have accomplished that which we set ourselves to accomplish. In no sense of hypocrisy we repeat our regret that such a step as we took was necessary.*
>
> *Sir Philip Ramon's death would appear to have been an accident. This much we confess. Thery bungled —and paid the penalty. We depended too much upon his technical knowledge. Perhaps by diligent search you will solve the mystery of Sir Philip Ramon's death —when such a search is rewarded you will realise the truth of this statement. Farewell.*

'It tells us nothing,' said the Commissioner.

Falmouth shook his head despairingly.

'Search!' he said bitterly; 'we have searched the house in Downing Street from end to end—where else can we search?'

'Is there no paper amongst Sir Philip's documents that might conceivably put you on the track?'

'None that we have seen.'

The chief bit the end of his pen thoughtfully.

'Has his country house been examined?'

Falmouth frowned.

'I didn't think that necessary.'

'Nor Portland Place?'

'No: it was locked up at the time of the murder.'

The Commissioner rose.

'Try Portland Place,' he advised. 'At present it is in the hands of Sir Philip's executors.'

The detective hailed a hansom, and in a quarter of an hour found himself knocking upon the gloomy portals of the late Foreign Secretary's town house. A grave manservant opened the door; it was Sir Philip's butler, a man known to Falmouth, who greeted him with a nod.

'I want to make a search of the house, Perks,' he said. 'Has anything been touched?'

The man shook his head.

'No, Mr Falmouth,' he replied, 'everything is just as Sir Philip left it. The lawyer gentlemen have not even made an inventory.'

Falmouth walked through the chilly hall to the comfortable little room set apart for the butler.

'I should like to start with the study,' he said.

'I'm afraid there will be a difficulty, then, sir,' said Perks respectfully.

'Why?' demanded Falmouth sharply.

'It is the only room in the house for which we have no key. Sir Philip had a special lock for his study and carried the key with him. You see, being a Cabinet Minister, and a very careful man, he was very particular about people entering his study.'

Falmouth thought.

A number of Sir Philip's private keys were deposited at Scotland Yard.

He scribbled a brief note to his chief and sent a footman by cab to the Yard.

Whilst he was waiting he sounded the butler.

136

'Where were you when the murder was committed, Perks?' he asked.

'In the country: Sir Philip sent away all the servants, you will remember.'

'And the house?'

'Was empty—absolutely empty.'

'Was there any evidence on your return that any person had effected an entrance?'

'None, sir; it would be next to impossible to burgle this house. There are alarm wires fixed communicating with the police station, and the windows are automatically locked.'

'There were no marks on the doors or windows that would lead you to believe that an entrance had been attempted?'

The butler shook his head emphatically.

'None; in the course of my daily duty I make a very careful inspection of the paintwork, and I should have noticed any marks of the kind.'

In half an hour the footman, accompanied by a detective, returned, and Falmouth took from the plain-clothes officer a small bunch of keys.

The butler led the way to the first floor.

He indicated the study, a massive oaken door, fitted with a microscopic lock.

Very carefully Falmouth made his selection of keys. Twice he tried unsuccessfully, but at the third attempt the lock turned with a click, and the door opened noiselessly.

He stood for a moment at the entrance, for the room was in darkness.

'I forgot,' said Perks, 'the shutters are closed—shall I open them?'

'If you please,' said the detective.

In a few minutes the room was flooded with light.

It was a plainly furnished apartment, rather similar in appearance to that in which the Foreign Secretary met his end. It smelt mustily of old leather, and the walls of the room were covered with bookshelves. In the centre stood a big mahogany writing-table, with bundles of papers neatly arranged.

Falmouth took a rapid and careful survey of this desk. It was thick with accumulated dust. At one end, within reach of the vacant chair stood an ordinary table telephone.

'No bells,' said Falmouth.

'No,' replied the butler. 'Sir Philip disliked bells—there is a "buzzer".'

Falmouth remembered.

'Of course,' he said quickly. 'I remember—hullo!'

He bent forward eagerly.

'Why, what has happened to the telephone?'

He might well ask, for its steel was warped and twisted. Beneath where the vulcanite receiver stood was a tiny heap of black ash, and of the flexible cord that connected it with the outside world nothing remained but a twisted piece of discoloured wire.

The table on which it stood was blistered as with some great heat.

The detective drew a long breath.

He turned to his subordinate.

'Run across to Miller's in Regent Street—the electrician—and ask Mr Miller to come here at once.'

He was still standing gazing at the telephone when the electrician arrived.

'Mr Miller,' said Falmouth slowly, 'what has happened to this telephone?'

The electrician adjusted his pince-nez and inspected the ruin.

'H'm,' he said, 'it rather looks as though some linesman had been criminally careless.'

'Linesman? What do you mean?' demanded Falmouth.

'I mean the workmen engaged to fix telephone wires.' He made another inspection.

138

'Cannot you see?'

He pointed to the battered instrument.

'I see that the machine is entirely ruined—but why?'

The electrician stooped and picked up the scorched wire from the ground.

'What I mean is this,' he said. 'Somebody has attached a wire carrying a high voltage—probably an electric-lighting wire—to this telephone line: and if anybody had happened to have been at——' He stopped suddenly, and his face went white.

'Good God!' he whispered. 'Sir Philip Ramon was electrocuted!'

For a while not one of the party spoke. Then Falmouth's hand darted into his pocket and he drew out the little notebook which Billy Marks had stolen.

'That is the solution,' he cried; 'here is the direction the wires took—but how is it that the telephone at Downing Street was not destroyed in a similar manner?'

The electrician, white and shaking, shook his head impatiently.

'I have given up trying to account for the vagaries of electricity,' he said; 'besides, the current, the full force of the current, might have been diverted—a short circuit might have been effected—anything might have happened.'

'Wait!' said Falmouth eagerly. 'Suppose the man making the connection had bungled—had taken the full force of the current himself—would that have brought about this result?'

'It might——'

' "Thery bungled—and paid the penalty," ' quoted Falmouth slowly. 'Ramon got a slight shock—sufficient to frighten him—he had a weak heart—the burn on his hand, the dead sparrows! By Heaven! it's as clear as daylight!'

*   *   *

Later, a strong force of police raided the house in Carnaby

Street, but they found nothing—except a half-smoked cigarette bearing the name of a London tobacconist, and the counterfoil of a passage ticket to New York.

It was marked *per RMS 'Lucania'*, and was for three first-class passengers.

When the *Lucania* arrived at New York she was searched from stem to stern, but the Four Just Men were not discovered.

It was Gonsalez who had placed the 'clue' for the police to find.

THE END

ORDER FORM

.... **ALLINGHAM:** Traitor's Purse	£2.95
.... **AMBLER:** Epitaph for a Spy	£2.50
.... **BLAKE:** The Sad Variety	£2.95
.... **BUCHAN:** Castle Gay	£2.50
.... **BUCHAN:** The Courts of the Morning	£3.50
.... **BUCHAN:** The House of the Four Winds	£2.50
... **BUCHAN:** The Power-House	£2.50
.... **CHARTERIS:** Enter the Saint	£2.50
.... **CHARTERIS:** The Saint in New York	£2.50
.... **CHILDERS:** The Riddle of the Sands	£2.50
.... **COLES:** Drink to Yesterday	£2.50
.... **HARLING:** The Enormous Shadow	£2.95
.... **HOPE:** The Prisoner of Zenda	£2.50
.... **HORNUNG:** The Collected Raffles	£3.50
.... **HOUSEHOLD:** A Rough Shoot	£2.50
.... **ROHMER:** The Mystery of Dr Fu Manchu	£2.95
.... **SAPPER:** The Black Gang	£2.50
.... **SAPPER:** Bulldog Drummond	£2.50
.... **SAPPER:** The Final Count	£2.95
.... **SAPPER:** The Third Round	£2.50
.... **WALLACE:** The Four Just Men	£2.95
.... **WALLACE:** The Mind of Mr J G Reeder	£2.50
.... **YATES:** Blind Corner	£2.50
.... **YATES:** Blood Royal	£2.50
.... **YATES:** Perishable Goods	£2.50
.... **YATES:** She Fell Among Thieves	£2.95

All these books may be obtained through your local bookshop, or can be ordered direct from the publisher. Please indicate the number of copies required and fill in the form below.

Name .... BLOCK
LETTERS
Address .... PLEASE

....

Please enclose remittance to the value of the cover price *plus* 40p per copy to a maximum of £2, for postage, and send your order to:
BP Dept, J.M. Dent & Sons Ltd, 33 Welbeck Street, London W1M 8LX

Applicable to UK only and subject to stock availability